Urbanization and Housing

State, Market and Consumer

Asish Mukhopadhyay

RAWAT PUBLICATIONS

Jaipur • New Delhi • Bangalore • Guwahati • Kolkata

ISBN 978-81-316-0819-7

Published by
Prem Rawat for **Rawat Publications**
Satyam Apts, Sector 3, Jawahar Nagar, Jaipur 302 004 (India)
Phone: 0141 265 1748 / 7006 Fax: 0141 265 1748
E-mail: info@rawatbooks.com
Website: www.rawatbooks.com

New Delhi Office
4858/24, Ansari Road, Daryaganj, New Delhi 110 002
Phone: 011 2326 3290

Also at *Bangalore, Guwahati* and *Kolkata*

Typeset by Rawat Computers, Jaipur
Printed and bound in India

To My Family

Contents

List of Tables and Graphs

Tables

Graphs

Acknowledgement

The present work has been possible as the Department of Consumer Affairs, Ministry of Consumer Affairs, Food and Public Distribution, Government of India, has been generous in providing necessary research grant. I take this opportunity to express my sincere gratitude to the Indian Institute of Public Administration, New Delhi, for awarding the present research project. I am particularly indebted to Professor Suresh Misra, Director, Centre for Consumer Studies, IIPA, New Delhi, and Professor Pranab Banerjee, Professor of Economics, IIPA, New Delhi, for their incessant encouragement and support at all stages of the project despite their busy schedule. I am grateful to the competent authority of my own institution for kindly permitting me to carry out the present research project simultaneously with my normal academic duties. I am indebted to my departmental colleagues for their stable academic support towards the implementation of the project. Thanks are due to the colleagues of some other departments of my own institution for showing keen interest about the study and for providing invaluable academic support. I am grateful to Professor Prasanta Ray, Professor Emeritus of Sociology, Presidency University, Kolkata for his helpful suggestions. I am extremely thankful to the officials of the State Consumer Disputes Redressal Commission (both in Bengaluru and Kolkata) for their kind co-operation in permitting me to use the available relevant authoritative data for the research project. Informal discussion with all of them had been of immense help. Indeed, they were more than co-operative. The research personnel, associated with the project, were very sincere and supportive.

The initial phase of fieldwork was crucial for more than one reason. Informal interactions with the 'consumers' provided invaluable insights into certain inadequately addressed issues. The respondent-consumer, who agreed to share his/her views on multiple issues, even knowingly, that the present researcher can't relieve him/her of undying property-related personal worries, deserves sincere thanks. The 'crisis of inter-personal trust' surfaced during the initial phase of fieldwork. I am not hesitant to admit that such 'critical negotiations' eventually turned out to be immensely useful methodological lessons.

I owe a lot to my family. It would have been extremely difficult for me to complete this work without ceaseless and unconditional support on behalf of my family. Interaction with my family encouraged me to take a look at the issues from perspectives not originally in my thought-process. Needless to add, the responsibilities for the observations made in the book are only mine.

Pranit Rawat of Rawat Publications (Jaipur) deserves sincere thanks for his consent to publish this piece of work.

Asish Mukhopadhyay

Introduction

Though teaching in Urban Sociology in India had its beginning as early as in 1919, interest in research on urban India grew much later barring individual initiatives. There had been a 'pronounced tilt' towards rural studies. Need for urban studies for a balanced image of the Indian society had been advocated by many scholars. A conspicuous move in scholastic interest towards urban studies is currently being witnessed. The 'urban turn' is gradually becoming prominent. It is probable that the visible changes in cities in tandem with authoritative reports on recent trends in urbanization in India and strong projections of various agencies about 'India's urban awakening' have weakened the 'entrenched perception of India as a land of villages' and have provided the necessary intellectual impetus for the 'urban turn'. The present initiative is intended to be an addition to this tradition of scholarship.

The sociologists become attracted to the process of urbanization and the city, in particular, for a variety of reasons and, of course, chiefly because, the city has always been the controlling centre of economic, political and cultural life, everywhere. As Wirth (1938: 2) argued:

> The influences which cities exert upon the social life of man are greater than the ratio of the urban population would indicate, for the city is not only in ever larger degrees the dwelling-place and the workshop of modern man, but it is the initiating and controlling center of economic, political, and cultural life that has drawn the most remote parts of the world into its orbit and woven diverse areas, peoples, and activities into a cosmos.

Davis (1955) identified four major reasons as to why the phenomenon of urbanization tends to become so attracted to the sociologists. The reasons are: first, the phenomenon of urbanization is relatively recent in human history; second, urbanization represents a revolutionary change in the whole pattern of social life; third, the cities, once established, tend to be the centre of power and influence throughout the whole society; and finally, many of the problems associated with the process of urbanization are unresolved; and consequently, its future directions and potentialities are still uncertain (Davis, 1955: 429). In so far as the Indian society is concerned, the phenomenon of urbanization, its promises and challenges, though exceedingly important, have failed to attract adequate attention of the sociologists, until recent times. That there had been a bias towards rural studies is generally agreed upon. This is despite that the need for urban studies for a balanced image of the Indian society had been advocated by many scholars. As Rao (1974), while arguing for the promotion of urban studies, observed:

> Our understanding of Indian social institutions has been largely based on the knowledge of village communities .... It is necessary to promote urban studies which would supplement the *rural view* and thus provide a balanced picture of Indian social institutions (Rao, 1974: 1).

The probable basis of 'pronounced tilt' for village studies in India may be found rooted deep in the practice of 'colonial representation of the village as the authentic expression of Indian civilizational values' (Nair, 2005: 5). As Kidambi (2007) puts it, it was the construct of nineteenth century colonial discourse that India had been a land of self-contained village communities. That the village was the authentic repository of timeless values and virtues of Indian civilization had been embraced by the elites of the time and this 'exerted a profound influence on their cultural and political imagination in the twentieth century' (Kidambi, 2007: 2).

Gandhi and Nehru, the leaders of the national movement and whose ideas strongly influenced the making of modern India, put thrust on taking sufficient care of the developmental needs of the villages in India. Gandhi strongly believed that 'India begins and ends in the villages', or, 'future of India lies in its villages'. It was in the thought-process of Gandhi, 'if the villages perish, India will perish too. It will be no more India. Her own mission in the world will get lost' (*Harijan*, 1936: 241). Nehru perceived 'increased urban migration and urbanization as alarming trends' and that it needed to be stemmed and reversed (Nair, 2005: 4). 'The fundamental problem of India being her villages', Nehru wanted 'to urbanize the village, not take away the people from the villages to towns' (Kalia, 1999: 30). Urbanization, to Nehru, was synonymous to modernization, 'which was expected to lift India out of the morass of the past and set it on the road to progress' (Prakash, 2002: 4). Also, Tagore had sufficient concern for rural reconstruction. Tagore strongly believed:

> If we could free even one village from the shackles of helplessness and ignorance, an ideal for the whole of India would be established .... Let a few villages be rebuilt in this way, and I shall say they are my India. That is the way to discover the true India.[1]

In 1922, Tagore took initiative to establish the institute of rural reconstruction in Sriniketan and his objective was:

> To bring back life in its completeness into the villages making them self-reliant and self-respectful, acquainted with the cultural tradition of their own country and competent to make an efficient use of modern resources for the improvement of their physical, intellectual and economic conditions (Bulletin, 1928).

However paradoxical it seemed, it was so that though most nationalist leaders had urban background and the cities were the major centres of nationalist activities, yet, 'the nationalist leaders looked to the village in defining India. The urban experience seldom received any concentrated attention. The city occupied an ambivalent position in the Indian nationalist imagination' (Prakash, 2002: 3). While elaborating on the relationship between Indian nationalism and city, Partha Chatterjee has also taken note of this paradoxical situation. As Chatterjee argues:

> The place of colonial modernity in India in the nineteenth and twentieth centuries was obviously the city and that is where India's nationalist elite was produced. Yet ... devoted most of their imaginative energies to the task of producing an idea not of the future Indian city but of a rural India fit for the modern age (Chatterjee, 2004: 140).

While suggesting a probable answer to this paradox, Chatterjee, argues:

> Perhaps lies in a perceived lack of agency by the Indian elite in thinking about the city .... The colonial cities of British India were largely creations of British colonial rulers to which Indians had adapted. There was, it seems to me, always a sense among the middle classes of the great colonial cities of India of not being in control of their surroundings .... Something of the popular attitude toward the big city as a deeply profane place, corrupted by money and commerce and littered with dangerously seductive amusements, was shared by the urban middle classes as well (Chatterjee, 2004: 140–41).

A recent study on Bombay in colonial India (1890–1940) reaffirms the view that 'the city occupied a central place in nationalist political practice' (Kidambi, 2012). If the city was so central to India's political modernity, the debate is rekindle, why did nationalist ideologues and activists devote so little energy to reimagining the city? Kidambi dispels the above-mentioned view of Chatterjee as 'unsatisfactory' and presents an alternative proposition for consideration:

> Perhaps it was because they were so irrevocably alienated from the village that the nationalist middle classes were able to make it an object of intellectual scrutiny and political reform. And conversely, perhaps it was because they had invested so heavily in the city and come to make it their own that nationalists had little inclination to rethink its future (Kidambi, 2012: 963).

The debate continues.

The dominant perception (that 'the defining feature of Indian society was its predominantly agrarian character') among the Indian elites had implications for the social research in India. The dominant perception not only 'tended to obscure the significance of its cities but also suffused the scholarship within the social sciences'. The anthropologists, the sociologists and the political scientists focused mainly 'on the countryside since the 'real' India was believed to reside, literally as well as figuratively, in her villages' (Kidambi, 2007: 2).[2]

Inadequate academic focus on urban situation in India may also be found related to the understanding of some social scientists who found no reason for urban studies 'since 80 per cent of the people lived in villages' (Rao, 1974: 1). Srinivas believed that 'village studies could form the basis for generalization about Indian social problems and process' (Srinivas, 1963). Srinivas, however, emphasized that it was urgent to undertake field-based studies on Indian villages, 'a type of society which is fast changing fundamentally and with great rapidity' (Srinivas, 1955).

As early as in 1919, teaching in Urban Sociology had its beginning in India (University of Bombay).[3] Generation of interest in research with respect to urban India however, took time. While there were individual academic initiatives on modern Indian city, 'the countryside continued to dominate the scholarly agenda in the 1970s and 1980s. Village studies revolving around caste, kinship and ritual held sway over the disciplines of Anthropology and Sociology' (Kidambi, 2007: 5). Saberwal, based on his overview of the studies on urban India in the late 1970s, discovered that 'sociologists and others have off and on referred to the urban phenomenon in India; but this terrain has until recently remained singularly devoid of decisive intellectual landmarks' (Saberwal, 1977: 1).

The ICSSR Survey of Advances in Research in Sociology and Social Anthropology in India (fourth in series), initiated in 2003 and completed in 2007, provides useful clues towards an understanding of progress of research in various (eleven) sub-fields[4] of Sociology and Social Anthropology in India. A three-year breakdown of the studies undertaken between 1988 and 2002 in those sub-fields of Sociology and Social Anthropology in India showed a significant increase in number of reported studies from 425 in 1988–90 to 972 in 2000–02. During the period under reference, the largest number of reported studies (1,450) had been undertaken in the field of Developmental Sociology (Atal, 2009: 14). It is surprising to note that total number of reported studies had been recorded below 100 in only two sub-fields during the aforesaid period. Those sub-fields were: Urban Sociology (79) followed by Demographic Transition (56). With respect to the sub-field of Urban Sociology, it was noted, that it could be that the studies carried out in newly-developed areas of specializations but in urban areas were not included under the sub-field of Urban Sociology and the resultant smaller number of reported studies in this Sub-area[5] (Atal, 2009: 19). The rural India continued to take precedence over urban India.

A conspicuous move in scholastic attention is, of late, being witnessed. The 'urban turn' is gradually becoming prominent (Prakash, 2002: 2). Scholars from various disciplines are being increasingly attracted to diverse issues related to urbanizing India and urbanization-induced socio-spatial transformation in Indian society in particular. Consequent upon softening of trade barriers between nations, the concomitant of economic globalization, the importance of city as the centre of business has increased manifold. The ICT revolution has allowed the cities across societies to become more integrated than ever before.

The twenty-first century India has been witnessing spatial expansion of urbanization, rapid expansion of the city-centric hi-tech service sector, 'a potent symbol of India's success in the global economy', emergence of 'hegemonic' middle class, intense drive towards 'internationalization' of the cities and proliferation of slums. It could be that these visible changes in cities in tandem with authoritative reports on facts of urbanization in India and projections of various agencies affirming India's 'urban awakening'[6] greatly weakened the 'entrenched perception of India as a land of villages' and provided the necessary intellectual impetus for the 'urban turn'.

Since the academics took cognizance of the 'urban turn', a significant number of critical studies have appeared with respect to urban India.[7] A glimpse of relevant studies reveals, while scholastic interest on various aspects of city and city life in colonial India or, 'colonial urbanism' continues unabated (for example, Chattopadhyay, 2005; Kidambi, 2007, 2012; Beverly, 2011; Spodek, 2013) academic interest related to the contemporary situation has also been distinctly growing. A few of recent studies with a focus on the contemporary context may be mentioned. For example, Ahluwalia (2014), Banerjee (2013) and Kundu (2009) have focused on urbanization and its challenges (and choices). The process of urbanization in large cities has been the focus of a good number of studies. To mention a few of these studies: Delhi (Ramkrishnan, 2013; Baviskar, 2003; Batra, 2009), Mumbai (Banerjee-Guha, 2009, 2002; Patel and Deb, 2009; Fernandes, 2004). It is not only the large cities, the state-sponsored 'New Towns' or, the Urban Centres (Dey et al., 2013; Bhattacharya and Sanyal, 2011; Shaw, 2003; Mitra, 2002) have also drawn attention of the scholars. Also, cross-cultural studies on cities with India as the empirical reference are emerging (Wang et al., 2010; Harris, 2008). Apart from mega cities, the scholars are being attracted to the smaller but happening cities like Bengaluru (Nair, 2005; Dittrich, 2007) and Ahmedabad (Spodek, 2011). These are 'twentieth century trajectory' of the respective city, aiming at tracing the rise of the respective city to the status of a metropolis.

These studies provide valuable inputs to our understanding of urban India through an analysis of diverse issues like contest over urban space for more 'productive' use, new urban middle class', exclusionary impact of urbanization and such other related issues. Apart from the academics, it will not be out of place to mention, there are research institutions and non-state or, not-for-profit organizations which are actively engaged in research related to urban India.

It is wrong to assume that the phenomenon of urbanization or, the city in particular, has been the exclusive domain of the sociologists. The scholars from other disciplines and in particular, geography, economics, architecture, anthropology and history have immensely contributed towards exploration, interpretation and understanding of the phenomenon of urbanization and urbanization-driven changes and challenges. In fact, the contributors to the body of literature of Urban Studies in India has been dominated by the geographers, economists, historians and other social researchers (Singh-Sandhu, 2004: 294; Nair, 2005: 5). This is corroborated by the trend in publication of articles on the subject in *Sociological Bulletin*, the official journal of the Indian Sociological Society (since its inception in 1952), which publishes mainly sociological studies (Singh-Sandhu, 2004: 294). Greater reciprocity between sociology and these disciplines is often advocated for a better understanding of the complex process of urbanism in India. As Jayaram observes:

> It is time that urban sociology looks outward, consciously crossing the disciplinary boundaries, though firmly located in the fundamentals of the parent discipline. This implies a willingness to work with practitioners of other disciplines, and openness to the methods, tools and techniques that they deploy in their approach to the city (Jayaram, 2009: 11).

Urbanization is relatively a new phenomenon in human history. Urbanization refers to a process that is spatial, temporal, diverse, continuous and complex. Historically, 'urbanization and the growth of cities have occurred together'. It could be that the cities were known to the people of early period of civilization. Urbanization was, however, not so widespread in ancient times. The 'urbanized' societies emerged later. As Davis noted:

> Although there were a few cities as early as 4000 BC, the cities of the ancient world were generally small and had to be supported by much larger rural populations. "Urbanized societies," in which a high proportion of the population lives in cities, developed only in the nineteenth and twentieth centuries. The process of urbanization has moved rapidly in the entire world since 1800 (Davis, 1955: 429).

What prevented the growth of large cities or, why even the small ones were few in number or, why the cities had to be supported by much larger rural population or, why the most advanced regions had not registered high degree of urbanization in early period of civilization? The major constraints to such development could be, Davis explains:

> Agriculture was so cumbersome, static, and labor-intensive that it took many cultivators to support one man in the city .... The instruments of production, to be sure, but clumsy. There were political limitations as well. Other limiting factors were the lack of scientific medicine (which made urban living deadly), the fixity of the peasant on the land (which minimized rural-urban migration), the absence of large-scale manufacturing (which would have derived more advantage from urban concentration than did handicraft), the bureaucratic control of the peasantry (which stifled free trade in the hinterland), and the traditionalism and religiosity of all classes (which hampered technological and economic advance) (Davis, 1955: 431).

It is generally believed that the growth of the non-agricultural economy or, industrialization and the resultant migration of population to the potential centres of opportunities facilitated the process of urbanization. It is common that the population engaged in non-agricultural activities dominates in an urban settlement, everywhere. However, the shift in occupation from agricultural to non-agricultural, it is often argued, is 'associated with urbanization but not identical with it' (Davis, 1965: 26). It is true that a noticeable change in urban growth was recorded during the nineteenth century. It is also true that the number of cities with 1,00,000 populations was evident well before the steam engine or the power loom had been invented. As well, London passed the million mark in population by 1810, before it had a mechanical means of transportation (Mumford, 1956). The debate over the basics to urbanization still continues.

Since urbanization is a continuous process, its 'future directions and potentialities remain uncertain'. Urbanization assumes change in lifestyle, attitudes, values, institutions, relationships besides principal source of livelihood. To be precise, urbanization demands a qualitatively distinct 'way of life' called urbanism (Wirth, 1938). A review of some recent academic initiatives, aiming at critically understanding the complex process of urbanization, reveals diverse tendencies embedded within the process of urbanization [*Exclusionary urbanization*[8] (Kundu, 2009), *Subaltern urbanization*[9] (Denis et al., 2012) and *Suburbanization*[10] (Ekers et al., 2012; Nijman and Clery, 2013) for example].

While debate continues over the status of the first city of the world with a million population (Rome or, London?), London became a city with at least one million inhabitants in 1800. By 1800, between 2 per cent and 3 per cent (data vary) of world population lived in urban areas. The proportion of world population, living in urban areas, increased from 2 per cent–3 per cent in 1,800 to 14 per cent–15 per cent in 1900. By the year 1950, the proportion of world urban population increased to 30 per cent. By the year 2000, about 49 per cent of total world population was urban. The second half of the twentieth century has been important for three major reasons: first, the urban population of the world grew by 2.1 billion; second, the pace of urbanization in developing countries (and more particularly in Latin America) has been spectacular; finally, the intensified global urbanization process has been accompanied by accelerated growth of mega cities and million-plus cities. While in 1950, New York was the only mega city (with a population of over 10 million), the number of mega cities has increased to 17 in 2000. The twenty-first century is expected to witness a shift in global urbanization pattern.

It is generally agreed upon that the twenty-first century will be both: an urban century and an Asian century and, much of urbanization will be happening in cities located in Asia (China and India). The urban population in Asia is expected 'to nearly double from 1.6 billion to 3.1 billion by 2050' (Table 1). Recent trends in urbanization in China 'reflects the global shift of the world's urban population from developed to developing countries'. In so far as India is concerned, urbanization has been taking place faster than anticipated. According to 2011 Census, the urban population has grown from 286.1 million (2001) to 377.2 million (2011) indicating an increase in the level of urbanization from 27.7 per cent in 2001 to 31.16 per cent in 2011. Again, for the first time since Independence, the absolute increase in population has been higher in urban areas than in rural areas. Also, the annual exponential rate of growth of 2.76 per cent registered during 2001–11 has reversed the declining trend registered during 1981–2001 (Bhagat, 2011; NIUA, 2011). It should be mentioned that India has the largest rural population (857 million) followed by China (635 million) in the world and these two countries together account for 45 per cent of the world's rural population. Also, rural population in both these countries is expected to decline in coming years. However, as in 2014, globally, more people live in urban areas (54%) than in rural areas (UN, 2014: 10). Between 2000 and 2050, urban population in Asia is expected to be double (ADB, 2011; Hugo, 2003; Mohan and Dasgupta, 2005; Peng et al., 2009). Again, 10 of the 17 global mega cities were in Asia between 1975 and 2000.

Table 1

Asia's Urban Population by 2050

Asia	*2010*	*2050*
Total Urban Population (in millions)	*1,649*	*3,247*
Northeast Asia	805	1,284
South Asia	496	1,261
Southeast Asia	252	520
Central Asia	96	182

Source: UN World Urbanization Prospects, 2007 Revision (ADB, 2011).

Of the 21 mega cities expected by 2015, 17 will be located in Asia. It needs to be mentioned that South Asia, compared to other sub-regions of Asia and the rest of the world, is amongst the least urbanized as around 69 per cent of its population reside in rural areas (Table 2). South Asia is, however, urbanizing at a rate greater than the rest of the world (Table 2A). Again, largely because of its large size and diversity, the trend in urbanization in South Asia is unevenly distributed (South Asia, 2014: 22–24). With China and India urbanizing rapidly, it is argued:

> The Asian urban century is truly here to dominate global development particularly given the fact that Asia's competitive strengths lie in sectors that are largely urban in nature, in manufacturing (especially in countries such as China, Bangladesh, India, Taiwan and Korea) and in service sectors such as information technology and information technology enabled services/business process outsourcing services in countries like India, Singapore and the Philippines' (Mohan and Dasgupta, 2005: 219).

Asia has a glorious past in terms of domination of global trade. Portugal pioneered the European trade with Asia towards the end of the fifteenth century, dominated the sixteenth century and declined in the seventeenth century (Table 3). Exports from Asia to Europe were heavily concentrated on pepper and spices but included silk, cotton, porcelain and other luxury goods too. West was flooded with Asian commodities. As trade between Europe and Asia grew, key ports became thriving commercial centres. Asia accounted for 58 per cent of the world's economy before the onset of the Industrial Revolution in the middle of the eighteenth century[11] (Maddison, 2006: 2; ADB, 2011: 15). The impact of European colonialism on Asia was modest until the nineteenth century. The 'domination of Asia' declined with the onset of the industrial revolution in the West. Asia's glorious past, in terms of its contribution to the world economy prior to the industrial revolution, has generated a debate as to what could be the appropriate expression to describe the situation in contemporary Asia?

Table 2

Rate of Urbanization in the World and South Asia 1950–2050

	Urban Population (Thousands)		*% of Total Population Living in Urban Areas*		*Annual Rate of Change Urban Population (%)*	
	World	*South Asia*	*World*	*South Asia*	*World*	*South Asia*
1950	7,45,495	73,541	29.4	15.6	–	–
1980	17,53,229	2,02,314	39.4	22.3	2.89	3.43
2010	35,58,578	4,98,348	51.6	30.6	2.39	3.05
2050	62,52,175	11,88,704	67.2	51.5	1.42	2.20

Source: Quoted from South Asia (2014).

Table 2A

Urban and Rural Population in the World by Regions, 2011

Region	*Urban (Thousands)*	*Rural (Thousands)*	*Total (Thousands)*	*% of the Total Population Living in Urban Areas*
North America	2,85,805	61,758	3,47,563	82.2
Latin America and Caribbean	4,72,175	1,24,454	5,96,629	79.1
Europe	5,39,010	2,00,289	7,39,299	72.9
Oceania	26,280	10,895	37,175	70.7
Asia	18,95,307	23,12,140	42,07,448	45.0
Asia	1, 60,711	76,146	2,36,858	67.9
East Asia	8,78,586	7,02,059	15,80,646	55.6
Southeast Asia	2,68,064	3,31,961	6,00,025	44.7
Central Asia	24,974	36,467	61,442	40.6
South Asia	5,11,309	1,1,42,369	16,53,679	30.9
Africa	4,13,880	6,32,043	10,45,923	39.6
World	36,32,457	33,41,579	69,74,036	52.1

Source: Quoted from South Asia (2014).

Table 3

Number of Ships Sailing to Asia from Seven European Countries, 1500–1800

	1500–1599	*1600–1700*	*1701–1800*
Portugal	1705	371	196
Netherlands	65[a]	1,770	2,950
England	–	811	1,865
France	–	155 1,300	
Other[b]	–	54 350	
Total	770	3,161	6,661

a 1590s.

b refers to ships of the Danish, Swedish and Ostend companies, but excludes Spanish ships trading with Asia via the Pacific from Acapulco.

Source: Bruihn, J.R. and Gaastra, F. (eds) (1993): *Ships, Sailors and Spices*, NEHA Amsterdam (as cited in Maddison, 2006: 1).

Some scholars have indicated their preference for the expression 'resurgence of Asia' to 'rise of Asia'. Lockard, for instance, prefers the term 'resurgence of Asia' and argues:

> I will argue that the recent rise of various Asian societies, and particularly China, represents a coming full circle, a return to a center stage in world affairs that they occupied earlier in world history. In this scenario, the resurgence of Asia represents not an aberration but continuity with the past (Lockard, 2012).

Also, Desai (2012: 1) observes in a similar tone:

> After a period of some 250 years in which Europe has been in the ascendancy, the economic pendulum has begun to swing back, 'back' because until about 1750 it was Asia that dominated the Eurasian land mass with its large cities, sophisticated lifestyles and flourishing trade. Then, Europe embraced the modernization of the industrial revolution and reaped the benefits.

It is wrong to assume that the 'thesis of urban explosion in Asia' is accorded uncontested appreciation. Asia's share in total number of migrants or incremental urban population, it is argued, 'reflects the impact of the rural and urban population base that are responsible for sending out and receiving these people'. Again, the sudden increase in number of cities beyond certain cut-off point implies that a good number of cities in Asia existed just below the cut-off point and those cities have crossed the cut-off point as the population growth in developing countries is higher compared to the developed countries due to natural and socio-cultural factors. Besides, it is likely that the less urbanized and the less developed continent of Asia will witness rapid urbanization. The concern for more orderly urbanization and better governance of the cities will induce the relatively developed and the larger countries to impose restrictions on migration (Kundu, 2009b: 46). Additionally, there is the apprehension of 'exclusionary urbanization'. It is possible that 'the state and city governments, being encouraged by positive association between the pace of urbanization and a few indicators of economic growth in recent years, would initiate more reform related to land, capital and labour which in turn would restrict entry of the poor and the unskilled migrants from rural areas and outside the country, especially those coming with their dependents, strengthening the process of exclusionary urban growth' (Kundu,

2009b: 46). Studies and reports on contemporary Asia are available to suggest that Asia has been experiencing rapid economic growth simultaneously with rising inequalities. The fact of rising inequalities along with rapid urban growth in Asia is duly reflected in the other view called 'economic dualism' or, 'two faces of Asia':

> One that is witnessed in the glitzy towers of Shanghai and Mumbai and the other seen in the gloom covering the slums of Jakarta, Manila, and Mumbai. This growing economic dualism poses a threat to sustaining Asia's dynamic growth and social cohesion (ADB, 2011: 52)

Reports are available to suggest that the 'glitzy tower' of the cities in Asia eclipses the surrounding slums (i.e. 'residential areas where dwellings are unfit for human habitation'). Manila or Mumbai is no exception. In fact, slum remains an undying feature of urban life across societies. The metros in India experience significant addition to slum population on regular basis. Proliferation of slums 'is not a result of sheer demographic shift. It is more a function of failing land and housing policies and delivery system than urbanization-driven demographic shift' (Slum, 2011: 8).

It is true that achieving the desired level of GDP depends to a great extent on the pace of urbanization (Bhagat, 2011). According to one estimate, 'the top 100 largest cities of India produce about 43 per cent of GDP with 16 per cent of the population and just 0.24 per cent of land area'. It is also true that failure to effectively integrate the excluded into the development process poses serious threat to 'sustaining Asia's dynamic growth and social cohesion'. It is often ignored that the thousands of urban poor, the victims of multiple deprivations, in Orangi (Karachi, Pakistan), Dharavi (Mumbai, India) and such other urban settlements across the continent of Asia are eligible for support against inequalities and exclusions in everyday life situation.

What constitutes an 'urban' area? Debate persists as to the defining criterion of 'urban'. As the definition of 'urban' varies between countries, a universal definition of what constitutes an urban area seems difficult. Attempt to use different criteria to define what is urban at different points of time by a country is not uncommon, either. The criterion (either or in combination), which most of the countries rely upon, in defining what is urban, are: (i) size of population; (ii) population density; (iii) built-up areas and distance between; (iv) proportion of population engaged in non-agricultural activities; (vi) legal and administrative status; and, availability of specific services (UN, 2005).

While some countries, for example, United Kingdom, Sweden and Brazil, use Built-up-Area (BUA) as the defining criterion of urban, some other countries, like Pakistan, Sri Lanka and Bangladesh define a settlement as urban based on an administrative criterion ('any settlement with Municipal Corporation, Municipality, Town Committee or Urban Council'). Nepal, on the other hand, defines urban exclusively in terms of size of population ('a settlement having at least 9,000 population'). Though a good number of countries use size of population as one of the significant criteria of urban, disagreement over definition of appropriate size (of population) continues (UN, 2005; Bhagat, 2005; South Asia: 2014). How is an urban area defined in India? It is best put in some detail.

In India, efforts to collect data on population may be traced back to the ancient times. Kautilya's *Arthashastra* has references to the methods of conducting population, economic and agricultural censuses and their relevance for formulation of policies of the state. Again, valuable information related to population, industry and wealth of the time of Emperor Akbar are found in *Ain-i-Akbari*. With the development of the modern system of government, accuracy of census data received greater attention. Census in England started in 1801. The British Parliament was keen to ascertain the population of the dependencies. Census of the city of Dacca by Henry Walters (1830) was 'perhaps, the first complete census of an Indian city'. Much later, in 1856, a decision was taken to undertake a general census of the population in India in 1861. The decision to undertake a general census was postponed because of the Great Mutiny (1857–58). Census on selected provinces (for example, North-Western provinces, Central Provinces) and cities (including Madras, Bombay and Calcutta) was, however, not interrupted. Upon initiatives of Lord Mayo, the Governor-General, the statistical organization became active. W.W. Hunter was appointed Director General of Statistical Survey in 1869. An effort was made during 1867–72 to undertake a census 'by the actual counting of heads as much as of the country as practicable'. The exercise, known as the Census of 1872, was 'neither a synchronous attempt nor covered all areas nor centrally supervised, moderated or compiled'. The first complete census of population had been conducted in 1881. Since 1881, the census of India is being regularly carried out every 10 years.[12] It will not be out of place to mention, while the first attempt to undertake census had to be postponed due to the Great Mutiny (1857–58), the 1921 and 1931 Censuses had been affected by the non-co-operation movement and sporadic political unrest, respectively. Again, the 1941 Census was interrupted because of the World War II (Raghavan, 2010).

An urban area, as defined by the colonial administration in India, included 'every municipality (irrespective of size); every cantonment; all civil lines (residential areas of officials) not included in municipal limits; and every collection of houses permanently inhabited by not less than 5,000 persons and of an urban character, though not under municipal government'. This definition was in force until 1951. The State Census Authority was authorized to apply its own mind in identification of a settlement as urban (Bhagat, 2005). Available data on number of towns/urban areas and proportion of urban population to total population (1901–1951) indicate that India witnessed a steady increase in number of towns/urban areas and in urban population (as percentage to total population) during the period (1901–51). The first decade of the twentieth century was an exception as it witnessed a fall in both respects (Table 4). Between 1881 and 1951, occupation of the population was not included as a criterion of identification of a settlement as urban. Interestingly, 'there was little change from 1881 to 1951 in the industrial structure of the Indian working force. The proportion of workers engaged respectively in agriculture, in manufacture, in trade and in other services, remained nearly stationary' (Thorner, 1962: 1156). Thorner added: 'agriculture (taken together with general labour) absorbed about three-quarter of the working force, and manufacture (with mining and construction) about one-tenth, while the remainder was halved by trade (with transport) and all other types of services' (Thorner, 1962: 1156). Corroborating Thorner, some other scholars noted that 'the Indian occupational structure showed little sign of change over the whole period 1881–1951' (Kumar and Raychaudhuri, 2013).[13] The Census Act was enacted in 1948. The first census, post Independence, had been undertaken in 1951.

Until 1951, as already stated, no change was made in the definition of urban. Census of 1961 introduced significant changes in the definition of town/urban areas. Presumably, these changes were intended to redefine the town/urban areas 'along the agricultural-industrial continuum'. All places (i) with an urban body like corporation, municipality, cantonment board or notified town committee, etc.; (ii) with a population of not less than 5,000; (iii) with a density of population of at least 400 persons per sq km (i.e.; 1,000 per sq mile) and, (iv) with at least 75 per cent of the working population engaged in 'non-agricultural' occupation were defined as urban area. Until it was modified in Census of 1981, livestock, forestry, fishing, hunting and plantations, orchards and allied activities were included as 'non-agricultural' occupation.

Table 4

Number of Towns, and Percentage and Growth Rate of Urban Population in India, 1901–1951

Census Year	*Number of Towns/Urban Areas*	*Urban Population (As Percentage of Total Population)*	*Annual Exponential Growth of Population*
1901	1,827	10.84	–
1911	1,815	10.29	0.03
1921	1,949	11.18	0.79
1931	2,072	11.99	1.75
1941	2,250	13.86	2.77
1951	2,843	17.29	3.47

Source: Kundu, Amitabh (2011b): 'Methods in Madness: Urban Data from 2011Census', Economic and Political Weekly, Vol. XLVI, No. 40, Oct 1, pp. 13–16.

While all other criteria of town/urban areas were retained, Census of 1981 introduced a couple of significant changes. These were: (i) only the *male* main working population would be taken into account and, (ii) the workers engaged in livestock, forestry, fishing, hunting and plantation, orchards and allied activities would *not* be counted as 'non-agricultural' workforce (Bhagat, 2005; Census of India). The intervening years witnessed the appearance of another concept viz.; Standard Urban Areas (SUAs) developed for the Census of 1971. It needs to be mentioned that the concept of SUAs replaced the Town Group concept of Census of 1961. The Town Group concept was abandoned upon severe criticism from the scholars at the International Geographical Union Congress held in 1968 in New Delhi (Ramchandran, 2012; Census of India).[14]

The identification of town/urban areas by the Census of India is based on a mix of administrative and demographic criteria. The town/urban areas are categorized as: Statutory Town (i.e.; 'an urban unit with a municipality, corporation, cantonment board or notified area committee') and Census Town (includes all other places satisfying the following criteria: (i) a minimum population of 5000; (ii) at least three-fourth (75%) of the male main working population engaged in non-agricultural pursuits; and (iii) a density of population of at least 400 (per sq km). In order to qualify as an urban area, all the three criteria (size, density and occupational structure) are required to be satisfied. The number of towns/urban areas has more than doubled (from 3,891 to 7,995) between 1981 and 2011. The impressive numerical growth in number of town/urban areas is a result of addition of 4,044 *Census Towns 'which are 'urban' by definition but 'rural' in governance'*. The increase has been phenomenal. Evidently, between 2001 and 2011, there has been an increase of 186.11 per cent of Census Towns. The unprecedented growth of Census Towns prompted the scholars, to inquire: 'could this be the result of some kind of census activism working under pressure to report a higher pace of urbanization?' (Kundu, 2011). Discontent continues over the defining criteria of an urban area as followed by Census of India. While Table 5 shows numerical growth of Census Towns in India between 1981 and 2011, the trend in urbanization in India (1961–2011) is shown in Table 6.

Table 5

Numerical Growth of Towns in India (1981–2011)

	Type of Towns		
Year	*Statutory*	*Census*	*Total*
1981	2,620	1,271	3,891
1991	2,922	1,693	4,615
2001	3,734	1,427	5,161
2011	4,041	3,894	7,435

Source: National Institute of Urban Affairs, JNNURM Directorate. (December 2011), Available at www.niua.org, www.indiaurbanportal.in; Sainath (2011);

Table 6

Trends in Urbanization in India (1961–2011)

Census Year	*Urban Population* (in million)*	*Percentage Urban*	*Annual Exponential Urban Growth Rate (%)*
1961	78.94	17.97	–
1971	109.11	19.91	3.23
1981	159.46	23.34	3.79
1991	217.18	25.72	3.09
2001	286.12	27.86	2.75
2011	377.10	31.16	2.76

* As the 1981 Census was not conducted in Assam, and the 1991 Census was not held in Jammu & Kashmir, the population of India includes projected figures for these states for those periods.

Source: Bhagat, Ram B. (2011): 'Emerging Pattern of Urbanization in India', *Economic and Political Weekly*, Vol. XLVI, No. 34, dated 20 August.

The administrative-demographic criteria, as used by Census of India, in identification of an urban unit, it is argued, are uncommon and unscientific and rigid application of these criteria leads to project 'low level of urbanization' in India. The occupational criterion of the population, required to qualify as an urban area, has attracted particular attention. While some scholars relate India's low level of urbanization to 'using a high level of non-farm employment as one of the tests, uncommon internationally?', some others argue for 'a broader view of urbanization and consider all kinds of activities (primary, secondary and territory) as legitimate urban activities'. The exclusion of women from the count of non-agricultural workers is disapproved as this allows 'gender bias into the definition of urban'. Besides, in absence of a 'standard definition of a Statutory Town', the chances of biased application of discretionary power by the competent authority, in matter of recognition or de-recognition to an area as urban, can't be ruled out. Apprehension is strengthened in a situation where the status of a 'Non-statutory Town' assures share of developmental grant and other advantages, not otherwise available (Bhagat, 2005; Denis et al., 2012; Denis and Marius-Gnanou, 2011, Ramchandran, 2012; Sainath, 2011; for example). What attributes to substantial increase in number of the 'Non-statutory Town' or, the 'Census Town'? Or, what prevents comparable numerical growth of the 'Statutory

Town'? Mention should be made that conferring the statutory (administrative) status to an area falls within the domain of the concerned state as the kind of statutory (administrative) status to be conferred to an area is exclusively governed by the state-level Municipal and Local Bodies Act. The decision of the state becomes influenced by a variety of considerations and chiefly economic.

Bhagat (2005), based on extensive research, argues: (1) a 'Non-Statutory Town' or, the 'Non-Municipal Town', as Bhagat calls it, becomes eligible for central assistance towards implementation of various schemes on rural development because of its non-statutory status. The assurance of central assistance on various developmental schemes allows the Non-Statutory Towns to survive without additional efforts towards mobilization of resources for own sake; (2) higher and varied tax and tariff levied in a Statutory Town acts as deterrent to change in status of an otherwise urban area; (3) living in a non-statutory city-fringe means 'living in close proximity to a city and access to its economy' without additional financial burden; (4) there is the real estate lobby to resist change in the status of a Non-statutory Town to avoid relatively stringent building rules applicable to a Statutory Town. Exerting pressure on the state for reversal of status of an area is not uncommon, either. Bhagat (2005) notes how 14 settlements within New Bombay and Thane municipal limits were 'officially "remade" villages'. The state of Haryana also followed the same path. A number of small municipalities were de-notified to bring these areas back under *panchayats* (Sivaramkrishnan, 2002).[15] Instances are there to suggest that the state often acts in haste the other way, i.e. becomes generous in granting the statutory status. The case of the state of Tamil Nadu is an example. Bhagat (2005) notes, hoping to attract investment, how the state of Tamil Nadu approved statutory status to a large number of areas in the 1990s as a strategy to boost its image as the most urbanized state in India.

It may be added, the state of West Bengal has the highest number of 'Census Towns' followed by Kerala. Between 2001 and 2011, the number of 'Census Towns' in the state of West Bengal has increased from 252 to 780. Reportedly, it is chiefly 'the paucity of fund that interferes with the process of up gradation of these "Census Towns". The state has not been considering to upgrade these "Census Towns" at this moment'.[16] The non-municipality status of these areas allows continued unplanned growth. As well, the inhabitants of these 'Census Towns' remain deprived of their legitimate right to basic civic amenities as enjoyed by their counterparts in municipal towns.

It is true that the decision of the state to confer or to withdraw or to deny the statutory status to an area is guided mainly by economic considerations. Truer it is, whatsoever the decision of the state, it is taken in an arbitrary manner. Again, the truly rural areas are deprived as the 'otherwise urban areas' become eligible for a share of central assistance meant for development of the rural areas. Moreover, the non-statutory status has discouraging effect for exploration of potentialities for mobilization of resources and the resultant surviving with 'dependency motivation'. Besides, the conservative approach of the state in exercising its prerogative in regard to conferring the status of a 'Statutory Town' allows generation of a misleading notion or, 'pessimistic perception' about urbanization in India (Algah, 2012). To be precise, the manner in which the state decides to identify the status of an area is arbitrary, unfair, discouraging and misleading.

Globalization has brought in unprecedented changes in cities, everywhere. It is not only the visibility but also the composition and the inner-life of cities have been experiencing rapid transformation. Opening up of the economies has made access to FDI easier in the housing and infrastructure sector. The global capital has been too keen to participate in the process of urban remaking in emerging economies including that of India. How does keen competition among the states to attract FDI (even with incentives) for 'internationalization' of the cities impact upon those who are at the lower end of income distribution? Is India experiencing signs of 'exclusionary urbanization'? Are the peripheries/city-fringes/suburbs growing? The global capital and urbanization have become intimately connected phenomena. Its consequences have become an inescapable reality of everyday life situation in steadily urbanizing societies of the Global South including that of India. The inadequately addressed perspectives of this inexorable reality call for critical examination.

The central concern of the first chapter (*Re-making Urban India: Some Reflections*) of the present book has been the process of remaking (remaking and reimagining has been used interchangeably) of urban India wherein the urban space has been the site of critical contest. The thrust of urban remaking is on the development of infrastructure of global standard and globalized spaces, to be precise, the 'World City'. 'The issue of local and global', it is argued, 'is found to intersect at this point whereby cities and their regions are converted into a globally designed space of economic regeneration as well as marginalization of a large segment that goes to unfold the dynamics of neoliberal urbanism ... across the country' (Banerjee-Guha, 2004: 19). Again, there is the developmental state, often coercive, to allow capital 'to overcome the barriers to accumulation'. The rural land is being transformed into urban space for its more 'productive use' often through 'capturing land from the low income population that may have lived there for many years'. Both, consent and compensation continue to remain contentious. A new form of governance that integrates the interest of capital and that of the state has been emerging disregarding or undermining the 'democratic' vision of the city and in the process, ruining the hope of an 'inclusive' city. The notion of urban is being redefined to allow 'the cities to emerge as geo-strategic points to further neo-liberalism in the Global South'. The city space is being reimagined keeping in mind the 'targeted consumers'; and 'to exclude those adjudged to be unsuitable and threatening whose class and cultural positions diverge from the 'targeted consumers' of the new space' (Banerjee-Guha, 2004: 17). Presumably, inherent in the process of reimagining of the urban space may be traced an element of either denial or displacement or dispossession or deception, everywhere.

The cities are marked by contrasts. The cities are the centres of opportunities as well as the centres of great risks or uncertainties. The cities are the centres of affluence as well as concentrations of poverty. They bring out the best in human enterprise as well as the worst in human greed. They contain some of the best social services available as well as host of many social ills like overcrowding, unsanitary living conditions, drug addiction, alienation, social unrest and environmental pollution (UNDP, 1990: 85). It is usual that the cities across societies witness transformative intervention in addressing the urbanization-induced challenges. During the late-nineteenth century (1859–65), the city of London introduced the sewerage and waste disposal system to contain deteriorating public health due to enormous growth in

London-based industries and metropolitan population. The beginning of the twenty-first century (2005) witnessed the launching of the largest urban planning initiative in independent India viz. the Jawaharlal Nehru National Urban Renewal Mission (JNNURM).[17] The Mission had been launched aiming at 'encouraging reforms and fast-track planned development of identified cities' with a focus on 'efficiency in urban infrastructure and service delivery mechanisms, community participation and accountability of urban local bodies, or parastatal agencies towards citizens'.

Under JNNURM, 1,517 housing projects and 2,815 infrastructure projects were approved between 2005 and 2011 (of these, 88% of the projects had been approved up to March 2009). The Performance Audit report of JNNURM by the Comptroller and Auditor General of India, however, reveals (as on 31 March 2011), only 22 of 1,517 (2.97%) approved housing projects for the poor were completed. During the same period, 231 of 2,815 approved infrastructure projects (36.17%) were completed (CAG, 2012–13). Housing and living conditions for the urban Low Income Households continue to be either inadequately available or uninhabitable or, unaffordable. The urban infrastructure projects get precedence over housing projects for the urban poor.[18]

Usual it is, urbanization leads to growth in demand for housing of all varieties (low-cost to high-end) surpassing the supply. Since Independence, urban housing received particular attention of the state. The post-reform years have witnessed significant shift in both: the priorities and the role of the state vis-à-vis the issue of urban housing. The end result has not been satisfactory. The chapter entitled: 'State and Urban Housing' reviews the policies and the priorities of the state in post-Independence India and the end result of its initiatives with particular focus on the 'affordable segment'. Housing for the urban marginalized in particular demands particular attention as urbanization in India has been taking place faster than anticipated.

The revolution in Information and Communication Technology (ICT) reinforced by the consensus for integration of the economies have facilitated the enterprises to aggressively promote a particularistic way of life (to be specific, 'gratification of desire') with their respective products and services. The taste, the preference, the choice, the aspiration, to be precise, the orientation to life and living of the urbanizing societies including that of India has become subject to rapid transformation. The chances of being victims of improper choice and fraudulent behaviour of the enterprises in everyday life have consequently increased, manifold. This necessitates greater attention to the issue of 'consumerism'.

'Consumerism', understood as the initiatives to protect the consumers against unethical and unlawful trade practices, is not a new phenomenon. It could be traced even in ancient India. Studies on ancient India suggest that the ancient India had initiated mechanism to protect the consumers against unfair trade practices. The British India witnessed enactment of certain crucial Acts to prevent unlawful and unethical business practices. The Sale of Goods Act, 1930, was the major protective law until the passage of the Consumer Protection Act, 1986. India, post-Independence, has enacted, repealed, replaced and amended Acts for protection of the consumers. Despite the long tradition of consumerism, a significant proportion of the consumers in contemporary India reportedly suffer from ignorance about the rights and the protective legislation. This seriously impedes the growth of consumerism. The approach of the business entrepreneurs towards consumerism is indeed crucial. The chapter titled: '*Consumerism in India: Evolution and Recent Trends*' concerns the initiatives to prevent fraudulent practices, the growth, role and challenges of the non-state consumer organizations, the state of consumers in contemporary India and such other related issues.

Desire for housing transcends time, class and culture. Empirical evidences are there to suggest that the home-buyers, in course of buying a property in the urban housing market, ordinarily experience a host of tricky practices which are neither avoidable nor acceptable to them. The number of 'registered disputes' do not actually reveal the magnitude of close encounters with such practices as these do not always mature as 'dispute' requiring formal institutional intervention. Response of the consumers to the issues is not uniform, either. The home-buyers (consumers) respond to these issues in three different ways. The tricky practices are either ignored or, negotiated or, contested by the victims of such practices. Individual difference in response to such practices is influenced by one's affordability to the loss/damage caused by deception and/or one's own assessment of self to tolerate the probable 'costs' associated with resolution through formal redressal mechanism. The consumers relate persistence of deception in the urban housing market to three probable sources viz. first; political patronization/tolerance to deceptive tendencies in the market; second, supply of housing units exceeds the growing demand; and third, state's limited success in enforcing rules to check irregularities in real estate segment. The chapter titled *'Urban Housing Market: Vulnerability and Choices of the Consumers'* attempts to explore the undying deceptive practices, the pattern of negotiation of the consumers with such practices and the probable sources of persistence of such practices in the urban housing market.

Urban housing sector remains a problematic area. On the one hand, there is chronic shortage of urban housing for all segments and the 'affordable segment' in particular. On the other, the home-buyers become vulnerable to unethical business practices in the housing market. It could be that unethical business practices are the function of chronic shortage of housing or, at least, chronic shortage of housing does not allow the unethical business practices to die out in the urban housing market. The issue of deception could be found related to governance and ultimately political will. The major stake-holders, to be specific, the state, the market and the consumer can initiate effective changes in reduction in shortage of housing of all varieties as well as incidence of fraudulent/unethical business practices in urban housing market. A set of viable strategies have been suggested in the concluding segment. The primary data, used in this book, have been drawn from two cities viz.; Bengaluru and Kolkata.

Notes

1. As quoted in 'Tagore and Rural Reconstruction', Debotosh Sinha, Muse India, the literary ejournal.
   http://www.museindia.com/focuscontent.asp?issid=33&id=2145
2. See also 'Introduction' in Nair (2005: 1–5)
3. Patrick Geddes, a sociologist and town planner from New Zealand, prepared over 50 'town planning' reports on Indian urban centres during his stay in India between 1914 and 1924. Geddes joined the newly created department of Sociology and Civics in the University of Bombay in 1919. Geddes emphasized on ecologically sensitive form of town planning for the urban environment in India. The influence of

Geddes was, however, restricted to a few individuals and did not have a lasting impact (Kidambi, 2007: 3; Nair, 2005: 5).

4. The 11 sub-fields included in the fourth Survey were: Tribal Studies, Rural and Agrarian Studies, Political Sociology, Urban Sociology, Industrial Sociology, Women's Studies, Demographic Transition, Indian Diaspora, Studies on Development, Criminological Studies and Sociology of Law (Atal, 2009: 4)
5. For details, see, Table 1.6 (Atal, 2009: 14–19).
6. It is estimated that by 2030, the urban population will increase to 590 million and the cities will account for nearly 70 per cent of India's Gross Domestic Product. The number of middle class households, earning between ₹ 2,00,000 and ₹ 1 million a year, will be around 147 million showing a fourfold increase (McKinsey, 2010, for example).
7. Bhowmik (2009), based on published articles and book reviews, has provided a brief but useful description of the relevant studies with respect to urban India published in selected journals between 1989 and 2002. The studies are distributed in 11 groups according to theme viz.; Cities, Urban Communities, Urban Policies and Processes, Urban Poverty, Urbanization and Health, Urban Violence, Slums and Urban Infrastructure.
8. Kundu (2009) argues that the process of urbanization in India is exclusionary in nature. The pattern of migration to cities in India suggests that there has been a decline in migrants moving in search of employment and an increase in business-related and study-related mobility. The in-built screening mechanism of the migration process prefers people from relatively high social and economic strata. The urban centres have become less accommodating to the poor, restricting their entry and the resultant increasing rural-urban inequality.
9. Denis et al. (2012) claims that the economically vital tiny settlements very well existed, whether or not, denoted urban by the Census of India. These exist independent of metropolis and autonomous in their interactions with other settlements, local and global. The growth of these settlements helps the rural poor in the vicinity apart from the urban poor. Again, the diversity and robustness of these settlements shows the myriad ways in which Indian citizens take their destiny into their own hands, often subverting patterns dictated from above.
10. The 'simple city-suburb dichotomy' is becoming gradually redundant as both are witnessing transformation and possibly everywhere. The scholastic debate over the issue of suburban governance continues. Based on the persisting debate on suburban governance (the modalities and mechanisms), Ekers et al. (2012) have differentiated the

three modalities: state, capital accumulation and private authoritarianism. Summing up the situation in US, Nijman and Clery has argued that the first couple of decades following the World War II witnessed increasing influence of government policies. 'With the onset of neo-liberalization in the early 1980s, private governance mushroomed, resulting in socio-economic differentiation at ever-finer scales. But neither the regulatory powers of the state nor the growing significance of non-governmental authority structures such as home-owner associations have in any way reduced the fundamental role of the market in US suburbanization' (Nijman and Clery, 2013: 19)

11. See also, Trade with Asia 1500–1800, Victoria and Albert Museum, London *www.vam.ac.uk/page/t/trade-with-asia–1500–1800*
12. For details, see 'Census of India-History of Indian Census', Office of the Registrar, General and Census Commissioner, GOI.
13. These scholars noted certain hidden changes. Between 1901 and 1951, 'factory employment expanded partly at the expense of non-factory employment; the more modern branches grew at the cost of a number of traditional ones ... associated with modernization under colonial rule ... in particular public, educational, medical and legal services' (p. 548).
14. What constitutes a Standard Urban Area and an Urban Agglomeration? The essential features of a SUA are: (i) it should have a core town of a minimum population size of 50,000; (ii) the contiguous areas, made up of other urban as well as rural administrative units, should have close mutual socio-economic links with the core town; and (iii) the probabilities are that this entire area will get fully urbanized in a period of two to three decades (Census of India). An Urban Agglomeration is defined as 'a continuous spread constituting a town and its adjoining urban Outgrowths (OGs) or two or more physically contiguous towns together and any adjoining urban outgrowths of such towns. Examples of OGs are railway colonies, university campuses, port areas, etc.; that may come up near a city or a statutory town outside its statutory limits but within the revenue limits of a village or villages contiguous to the town or city. Each such individual area by itself may not satisfy the minimum population limit to qualify it to be treated as an independent urban unit but may deserve to be clubbed with the town as a continuous urban spread' (Census of India).
15. As quoted in Bhagat, 2005 (p. 65)
16. As reported in *Ananda Bazar Patrika* (a vernacular daily published from Kolkata) dated 25 August 2013.
17. The Project had been launched in 63 mission cities. These include: the seven metropolitan cities with four million plus population as per

2001 Census, 28 cities with more than one million plus but less than four million population as per 2001 Census and 28 selected cities that were State capitals or had historic, religious or tourist importance. Two more cities were added to the set of mission cities taking the total to 65 cities. The Mission consists of two kinds of reforms: Mandatory (at the Level of ULBs, and Parastatal Agencies) and Optional (common to States, ULBs and Parastatal Agencies). The Mission envisages an investment of more than ₹ 1,00,000 crore with a central share of nearly ₹ 66,084 crore (as revised in 2009). For details, see JNNURM Overview, http://jnnurm.nic.in

18. The said report by the Comptroller and Auditor General of India noted irregularities of various kinds, including violation of norms prescribed for construction, the risk of ineligible beneficiaries deriving benefits of this scheme, unsuitable supporting infrastructure and living condition, diversion of funds for purposes other than those admissible under JNNURM. For details see, 'Implementation of Housing Projects' (pp. 1–17).
http://saiindia.gov.in/english/home/Our_Products/Audit_Report/Government_Wise/union_audit/recent_reports/union_performance/2012_2013/Commercial/Report_15/Report_15.html

References

ADB (2011): ASIA 2050, Realizing the Asian Century, Asian Development Bank, Phillippines.
http://www.aabcouncil.com/files/1772738/uploaded/ADB_Report_on_The_Asian_Century_%28asia-2050%29.pdf

Ahluwalia, Isher Judge ed. (2014): *Urbanization in India: Challenges, Opportunities and The Way Forward*, Sage Publications, New Delhi.

Alagh, Yoginder K. (2012): 'Census Towns Behind India's Missing Urbanization', *The Financial Express*, 6 April.

Atal, Yogesh (2009): *Sociology and Social Anthropology in India* (ICSSR Survey of Advances in Research), Indian Council of Social Science Research, New Delhi.

Banerjee, Anuradha ed. (2013): *Contemporary Urbanization in India: Issues and Challenges*, Concept Publishing, New Delhi.

Banerjee-Guha, Swapna (2009): 'Neoliberalising the "Urban": New Geographies of Power and Injustice in Indian Cities', *Economic and Political Weekly*, Vol. 44 (22), pp. 95–107.

Banerjee-Guha, Swapna (2002): 'Shifting Cities: Urban Restructuring in Mumbai', *Economic and Political Weekly*, Vol. 37 (2), pp. 121–128.

Banerjee-Guha, Swapna (2004): 'India's New Economic Policy and Contemporary Urban Planning, Socio-Spatial Injustices in Mumbai's

Redevelopment', 'Creative Destruction and the New Geographies of Empire', Conference held at the Centre for Place, Culture and Politics, City University of New York in April, pp. 9–21.
http://www.udri.org/udri/MumbaiReader09/01%20Swapna%20Banerjee%20Guha%20%20India%92s%20New%20Urban%20Policy%20&%20Contemporary%20Urban%20Planning.pdf

Baviskar, Amita (2003): 'Between Violence and Desire: Space, Power, and Identity in the Making of Metropolitan Delhi', *International Social Science Journal*, Vol. 55, Issue 175, pp. 89–98, March.

Batra, Lalit (2009): *A Review of Urbanization and Urban Policy in Post-independent India*, Working Paper Series, Centre for the Study of Law and Governance, Jawaharlal Nehru University.

Beverly, Eric Lewis (2011): 'Colonial Urbanism and South Asian Cities', *Social History*, 36: 4, pp. 482–497.

Bhagat, Ram B. (2011): 'Emerging Pattern of Urbanization in India', *Economic and Political Weekly*, Vol. XLVI, No. 34, dated 20 August, pp. 10–12.

Bhagat, Ram B. (2005): 'Rural-Urban Classification and Municipal Governance in India', *Journal of Tropical Geography*, 26(1), pp. 61–73.

Bhattacharya, Rajesh and Sanyal, Kalyan (2011): 'Bypassing the Squalor: New Towns, Immaterial Labour and Exclusion in Post-colonial Urbanization', *Economic and Political Weekly*, Vol. XLVI, No. 31 July 30.

Bhowmik, Sharit (2009): 'Urban Sociology' in *Sociology and Social Anthropology in India*, Yogesh, Atal ed.(2009), ICSSR Survey of Advances in Research, ICSSR, New Delhi, pp. 237–63.

Bulletin (1928): 'Aims and Objects', *Visva-Bharati Bulletin*, No. 11 (December 1928). p. 1. (as quoted in 'Tagore and Rural Reconstruction', Debotosh Sinha, Muse India, the literary ejournal).
http://www.museindia.com/focuscontent.asp?issid=33&id=2145

CAG (2012–13): Performance Audit on Jawaharlal Nehru National Urban Renewal Mission, Comptroller and Auditor General of India, GOI.
http://saiindia.gov.in/english/home/Our_Products/Audit_Report/Government_Wise/union_audit/recent_reports/union_performance/2012_2013/Commercial/Report_15/Report_15.html

Census of India (2011): 'Rural Urban Distribution of Population (Provisional Population Totals)', Registrar General and Census Commissioner, India, Ministry of Home Affairs, New Delhi.

Census of India: 'Census of India-History of Indian Census', Registrar General and Census Commissioner, GOI.
www.censusindia.gov.in/Data_products/Library/Indian_perceptive_link/History_link/census

Chattopadhyay, Swati (2005): *Representing Calcutta: Modernity, Nationalism, and the Colonial Uncanny* (Asia's Great Cities; Asia's Transformations) Routledge, New York: London.

Chatterjee, Partha (2004): *The Politics of the Governed, Reflections on Popular Politics in Most of the World*, Columbia University Press, NY [see also, Kidambi, Prashant (2012)].

Davis, Kingsley (1965): 'Urbanization of Human Population' in *City Reader*, Richard T. LeGates and Frederic Stout (ed.), 5th edition (Part–1, pp. 20–30).

Davis, Kingsley (1955): 'The Origin and Growth of Urbanization in the World', *American Journal of Sociology*, Vol. 60, No. 5, March, pp. 429–37.

Denis, Eric et al. (2012): 'Subaltern Urbanization in India', *Economic and Political Weekly*, (Review of Urban Affairs), Vol. XLVII, No. 30, pp. 52–62.

Denis, Eric and Kamala Marius-Gnanou (2011): 'Toward a Better Appraisal of Urbanization in India' cyburgeo.revues.org/24798, DOI: 10.4000/cybergeo.24798.

Desai, Meghnad (2012): 'The Resurgence of Asia', *Asian Affairs*, Vol. 43, Issue 1, pp. 1–11.

Dey, Ishita, Samaddar, Ranabir, Sen, Suhit K (2013): *Beyond Kolkata Rajarhat and the Dystopia of Urban Imagination*, Routledge, New Delhi.

Dittrich, Christopher (2007): 'Bangalore: Globalization and Fragmentation in India's Hightech-Capital', *ASIEN* 103 (April), S. pp. 45–58.

Fernandes, Leela (2004): 'The Politics of Forgetting: Class Politics, State Power and the Restructuring of the Urban Space in India', *Urban Studies*, Vol. 41, No. 12, November, pp. 2415–2430.

Gooptu, Nandimi (2001): *The Politics of the Urban Poor in Early Twentieth Century India,* Cambridge University Press, Cambridge.

Harris, A (2008): 'From London to Mumbai and Back Again: Gentrification and Public Policy in Comparative Perspective' (eprints.uci.ac.uk/14811/1/14811.pdf).

Ekers, Michael, Hamel, Pierre and Keil Roger (2012): 'Governing Suburbia: Modalities and Mechanisms of Suburban Governance', *Regional Studies*, Vol. 46. Issue 3, March, pp. 405–22.

Harijan (1936): 'Gandhi on Villages', Selected and Compiled with an Introduction by Joshi, Divya: 2002, (see Introduction).
http://www.mkgandhi.org/gandhionvillages/intro.htm.

Hugo, Graeme (2003): 'Urbanization in Asia: An Overview', University of Adelaide, Australia.

Jayaram, N. (2009): 'Revisiting the City: The Contemporary Relevance of Urban Sociology'. Paper presented at the Conference on 'Urban

Aspiration in Global Cities', Max Plank Institute for the Study of Religious and Ethnic Diversity, Gottingen, 9–11 August.

Kalia, Ravi (1999): *Chandigarh: The Making of an Indian City*, Oxford University Press, Delhi (as quoted in Prakash, Gyan (2002), p. 4).

Kidambi, Prashant (2012): 'Nationalism and the City in Colonial India: Bombay, c.1890–1940', *Journal of Urban History*, 38(5), pp. 950–967.

Kidambi, Prashant (2007): *The Making of an Indian Metropolis, Colonial Governance and Public Culture in Bombay, 1890–1920*, Ashgate, England and USA.

Krishna, Sudhir (2013): 'Transformative Impact of JNNURM', PIB (Press Information Bureau) Feature.
http://pib.nic.in/newsite/efeatures. aspx?relid=91801.

Kumar, Dharma and Raychaudhuri, Tapan (2013): *The Cambridge Economic History of India*, Vol. II, C. 1757–2003, Orient BlackSwan, New Delhi.

Kundu, Amitabh (2009): 'Exclusionary Urbanization in Asia: A Macro Overview', *Economic and Political Weekly*, Vol. XLIV, No. 48, 29 November (see also, Kundu, Amitabh (2012): 'Migration and Exclusionary Urbanization in India', *Economic and Political Weekly*, Vol. XLVII; 30 June).

Kundu, Amitabh (2009 b): 'Urbanization and Migration: An Analysis of Trend, Pattern and Policies in Asia', *Human Development Research Report* 2009/16 (UNDP).

Kundu, Amitabh (2011): 'Trends and Progress Of Urbanization, Human Settlement Group', IIED, Population and Development Branch, UNFPA, p. 8.

Kundu, Amitabh (2011b): 'Methods in Madness: Urban Data from 2011Census', *Economic and Political Weekly*, Vol. XLVI, No. 40, Oct 1, pp. 13–16.

Lockard, Craig A. (2012): 'The Asian Resurgence in World History Perspective', *World History Connected*, Vol. 9, No. 1, (Special Issue on Re-conceptualising Asia in World History).
www.worldhistory connected.press.illinois.edu/9.1/lockard.htm)

McKinsey (2010): India's Urban Awakening: Building Inclusive Cities, Sustaining Economic Growth, McKinsey Global Institute, (Delhi, Chennai, Mumbai), Mckinsey & Company.

Maddison, Augus (2006): 'Asia in the World Economy 1500–2030 AD', *Asian-Pacific Economic Literature*, The Australian National University and Blackwell Publisher Asia Pvt. Ltd.

Mitra, Sanjay (2002): 'Planned Urbanization through Public Participation: Case of the New Town, Kolkata', *Economic and Political Weekly*, 37 (11), pp. 1048–54.

Mohan, Rakesh and Dasgupta, Subhagato (2005): 'The 21st Century: Asia Becomes Urban', *Economic and Political Weekly*, 15 January, pp. 213–23.

Mumford, Lewis (1956) 'The Natural History of Urbanization' *in* William L. Thomas, jr. (ed.), *Man's Role in the Changing the Face of the Earth*, University of Chicago Press (1956), Chicago and London. http://habitat.aq.upm.es/boletin/n21/almum

Nair, Janaki (2005): *The Promise of the Metropolis: Bangalore's Twentieth Century*, Oxford University Press (Paperback Edition).

Nijman, Jan and Clery, TOM (2013): *Suburban Imaginaries and Metropolitan Realities in North America*, Working Paper Series (October), Centre for Urban Studies, University of Amsterdam.

NIUA (2011): India's Urban Demographic Transition, National Institute of Urban Affairs, New Delhi.

Patel, Sujata and Deb, Kushal (2009): *Urban Studies*, Oxford University Press, New York.

Peng, Xizhe et al. (2009): 'Urbanization and its Consequences' *Encyclopedia of Life Support Systems* (EOLSS), Demography (Vol. II).

Prakash, Gyan (2002): 'The Urban Turn', in *The Cities of Everyday Life*, Sarai Reader 02, pp. 2–7, Delhi.

Raghavan, P. (2010): 'Column: Brief History of Census of India', *The Financial Express*, 2 April.

Ramakrishnan, Kavita (2013): 'City Futures: Aspirations and Urban Imaginaries in Delhi', *Kaleidoscope 5*. 1 January, pp. 100–108 (Institute of Advanced Study, Durham University).

Ramchandran, R. (2012): *Urbanization and Urban Systems in India*, OUP Paperbacks, Delhi.

Rao, M.S.A. (ed.) (1974): *Urban Sociology in India: Reader and Source Book*, Orient Longman, Hyderabad (as quoted in Nair, Janaki, 2005).

Saberwal, Satish (1977): 'Indian Urbanism: A Socio-historical Perspective', *Contributions to Indian Sociology*, Vol. 11, No. 1, pp. 1–19.

Sainath, P. (2011): 'Census Finding Point to Decade of Rural Distress', *The Hindu*, 26 September.

Shaw, Annapurna (2003): 'Urban Growth, Basic Amenities and Waste Management in India' in Ramaprasad Sengupta and Anup K. Sinha (ed.) *Challenges of Sustainable Development: The Indian Dynamics*, Manak Publications, New Delhi, pp. 298–338.

Singh-Sandhu, Ravinder (2004): 'Half a Century of Urban Sociology in India', in Surendra Kumar Gupta (ed.), *Emerging Social Sciences Concerns: Fetschrift in Honour of Professor Yogesh Atal*, Concept Publishing Company, New Delhi, pp. 289–98.

Sivaramkrishnan, K.C. (2002): 'Turning Urban, Staying Rural', *The Hindu*, 27 February, [as quoted in Bhagat, Ram B (2005)].

Slum (2011): Report of the Working Group on Urban Poverty, Slums and Service Delivery System, Steering Committee on Urbanization, Planning Commission, New Delhi, p. 8.

Spodek, Howard (2013): 'City Planning in India under British Rule', *Economic and Political Weekly*, 48 (4), pp. 53–8.

Spodek, Howard (2011): *Ahmedabad: Shock City of Twentieth-Century India*, Indiana University Press, Bloomington.

Soja, E. and Kanai, M. (2007): 'The Urbanization of the World' in R. Burdett and D, Sudjic (eds.), *The Endless City*, Phaidon, London (as quoted in Peng, Xizhe et al. (2006).

South Asia (2014): 'Human Development in South Asia, Urbanization: Challenges and Opportunity', 17th Annual Report, Mahbub ul Haq Centre, Lahore, Pakistan.
http://mhhdc.org/wpcontent/themes/mhdc/reports/SAHDR_2014_Urbanization_Challenges_and_Opportunities.pdf

Srinivas, M.N. (ed.) (1963): *India's Villages*, Asia Publishing House, Bombay (as quoted in Nair, Janaki, 2005: 4).

Srinivas, M.N. (1955): 'Village Studies and their Significance' in Majumder D.N. (ed.), *Rural Profiles* (1) (Ethnographic and Folk Culture Society, Lucknow) as quoted in Nair, Janaki (2005: 4).

Thorner, Alice (1962): 'The Secular Trend in the Indian Economy, 1881–1951', *The Economic Weekly*, Special Number, July pp. 1156–65.

UN (2014): World Urbanization Prospects, The 2014 Revision, United Nations, New York.

UN (2005), 'Definition of 'Urban', *Demographic Yearbook 2005*, (Table 6) United Nations, New York.

UNDP (1990): Human Development Report, United Nations Development Programme (UNDP), New York, Oxford University Press.

Wang, Lan, Kundu, Ratoola and Xianming, Chen (2010): 'Building for What and Whom? New Town Development as Planned suburbanization in China and India' in *Suburbanization in Global City*, Mark Clapson and Ray Hutchison (ed), Emerald, UK, pp. 319–45.

Wirth, Louis (1938): 'Urbanism as a Way of Life', *American Journal of Sociology*, Vol. 44, No. 1, July, pp. 1–24.

CHAPTER 1

Remaking Urban India

Some Reflections

The urban space has become the site of critical contest. The cities across societies are witness to a spate of real estate activities and fierce battle for gaining control over the urban space to redevelop it for more 'productive' use. The global and the local 'intersect to eliminate the obstacles to urban redevelopment'. The 'new liberalizing middle class' and the state are engaged in a 'politics of forgetting' to displace the urban marginalized from such spaces ruining the hope of an 'inclusive' city. Again, there is the 'developmental' state's intervention, often coercive, into the accumulation process. The rural land is being transformed into urban space often through 'capturing land from the low income population that may have lived there for many years'. Presumably, inherent in the process of urban remaking may be traced an element of either denial or deception or displacement or dispossession, everywhere.

Introduction

Neo-liberalism argues for a limited state, private property, privatization of social resources apart from weakening of regulatory norms to the advantage of free market (Mirô, 2011: 2). The forms of neo-liberalism have, however, undergone changes, overtime, in terms of role of state from a limited or a reduced state to a state actively engaged in advancing the interest of capital, in particular.

'The logic of building cities upon dynamics of global financial capitalism has given rise to the view what is known as neoliberal urbanism' (Mirô, 2011: 2). Capital look to urban transformation as 'a major channel of absorption of surplus capital'. As Harvey (2008) argues, 'urbanization has played a particularly active role ... in absorbing the surplus product that capitalists perpetually produce in their search for profits'. This has been done specifically by 'restructuring, urban expansion, and speculation' (Mirô, 2011). Surplus absorption through urban transformation, at ever increasing geographical scale, 'has been possible through 'creative destruction', which nearly always has a class dimension. It is because the poor, the underprivileged and those marginalized from political power that suffer first and foremost from this process' (Harvey, 2008). The cities have become the strategically important arenas in which the neo-liberalizing forms of 'creative destruction' have been unfolding (Peck et al., 2009: 57).

The production of the city, within the framework of neo-liberal urbanism, produces new spatial, social, and power relations (Swyngedouw et al., 2002). Urban elites dominate the process of policy-making in regard to urban restructuring. Urban policies are designed to the advantage of capital and not for the sake of the citizens. Public-private partnership becomes a new form of governance. The cities become central to the very reproduction, extension and mutation of neo-liberalism itself. Indeed, a marked 'urbanization of neo-liberalism' has been occurring as 'cities become strategic targets and proving grounds for an increasingly broad range of neoliberal policy experiments, institutional innovations and political projects' (Peck et al., 2009: 65).

Studies and reports on cities across societies suggest that the urban space has become the site of critical contest. The cities have been witnessing a spate of real estate[1] activities and fierce battle for gaining control over the urban space to redevelop it for more 'productive' use. The global and the local 'intersect to eliminate the barriers to urban redevelopment'. The liberalization of economies, the concomitant of the process of economic globalization, has reinforced the process of accumulation by way of allowing the global capital to remake the cities. Again, there is the 'developmental' state's intervention, often coercive, into the accumulation process. The intervention of the state to allow capital 'to overcome the barriers to accumulation' has generated scholastic disagreement over the essence of the process of capital accumulation under neo-liberalism. It is being debated whether or not the process of accumulation by dispossession be construed as a 'decidedly political' process rather than a 'primarily economic' process. Urban remaking appears with altogether different meaning to the 'two contending forces, the corporate and the democratic, which claim stake over the city'. These forces continue to contend over pursuance of respective interest. Aggressive promotion of the urban real estate sector for 'internationalization of the cities' produces a highly fragmented and polarized urban society.

These and such other observations related to the critical process of urbanization provided primary stimulus in drawing up the framework of the present chapter. The thrust of the present chapter has been: the process of socio-spatial transformation of cities, 'commodification' of rural land, the position taken by the 'new liberalizing middle class' vis-à-vis restructuring of urban space and exclusionary impacts of urbanization. The particular focus has been the Indian society.

Urban Remaking I

The cities across societies are witnessing unprecedented changes in terms of reuse of urban space. Encouraged by the reform of the economy, the cities in India, not alone the mega cities, are desperately trying to transform themselves into the preferred destination of the private investors, and the global investors, in particular. The thrust of urban restructuring or redevelopment or remaking has been on the development of infrastructure and 'globalised spaces'. The over-accumulated global financial institutions, in a desperate quest for newer outlets, have been too willing to invest in real estate sector. The soaring Foreign Direct Investment (FDI) in real estate sector in contemporary India is at least, indicative of a couple of trends: first, the pace at which the cities in India are being redeveloped and second, the interest and involvement of the global financial institutions with the process of urban redevelopment in contemporary India. Between April 2000 and September 2014, the construction development sector received about $24 billion, constituting 10 per cent of the overall FDI into the country during the period until FDI inflow into the real estate sector started slowing down since 2012–13 (Table 7 and Table 8). An apprehension of further decline in inflow of FDI into this sector, certain changes in the norms governing FDI, has been introduced. The norms, governing FDI in construction sector, have been eased much in keeping with the demands of the real estate sector. The norms related to lock-in period and minimum floor area requirement have been relaxed. For a project, to become eligible for FDI, the minimum floor area required has been reduced to 20,000 sqm from 50,000 sqm and capital requirement has been halved to $5 million from $10 million. The foreign *developers* shall now be allowed to exit a project only after completion or after completing the basic trunk infrastructure such as roads, water supply, street lighting, drainage and sewage. Besides, an allocation of ₹ 7,060 crores has been announced for the development of 100 smart cities across the country. Moreover, an allocation to the tune of ₹ 4,000 crore has been made for developing low-cost housing, along with ₹ 50,000 crore for urban housing (*Business Standard*, 2014). It is true that relaxation of FDI norms in construction sector will give boost to this sector. It is, however, apprehended that it may inflate the urban housing bubble (Chadah: 2014). Until recent past, investment was going on in the outskirts of the cities because locating an area of 50,000 sqm. within the city, for the purpose of development/construction, had been somewhat difficult. The relaxed norms related to minimum floor area would now allow development of smaller projects, especially within the city, where the availability of land for construction is limited. Again, there is no reason to believe that the price of property will come down to the advantage of the prospective home-buyers with more investment for construction within the city. It is simply because demand for houses in posh localities far exceeds supply and the builders will now be encouraged more to cater the requirement of high-end variety than building 'affordable' housing. Further, speculation in urban real estate will increase as investors will seek to secure high return on investment. Speculation in real estate will spread to smaller towns, as well.

Table 7

*Statement on Sector-wise FDI Equity Inflows**
April 2000–October 2012

S. No.	*Sector*	*Amount of FDI Inflows*		
		In ₹ (Crore)	*In US $ (Million)*	*% With Total FDI Inflows (+)*
1.	Service Sector (Fin., Banking Insurance, Non-Finance/Business Outsourcing, R&D, Courier, Tech. Testing and Analysis, Others)	1,65,367.32	39,952.04	19.37

Cont'd...

...Cont'd

2.	Construction Development (township, built-up infrastructure and construction development projects)	97,510.90	21,430.16	11.34
3.	Tele-communications	57,342.53	12,600.57	6.79
4.	Computer Software and Hardware	51,494.71	11,456.48	6.17
5.	Drugs and Pharmaceuticals	45,934.77	9,775.03	5.27

* Top Five Sectors.

Source: 'Fact sheet on Foreign Direct Investment (FDI)', Department of Industry Policy and Promotion, Ministry of Commerce and Industry, GOI, Available at www.dipp.nic.in

Table 8

Statement on Sectors Attracting Highest FDI Equity Inflows (2010–11 to 2012–13)*

S. No.	*Sector*	*Amount in ₹ Crores (in US$ million)*				
		2010–2011 (April-Mar)	*2011–2012 (April-Mar)*	*2012–2013 (April-Mar)*	*Cumulative Inflows (April '00–Oct '12)*	*% to total inflows (in terms of US$)*
1.	Service Sector (financial and non-financial)	15,053 (3,296)	24,656 (5,216)	19,595 (3,600)	1,65,368 (35,952)	19%
2.	Construction Development (townships, housing, and built-up infrastructure)	7,552 (1,688)	15,236 (3,141)	3,748 (691)	97,511 (21,430)	12%
3.	Tele-communications (radio paging, cellular mobile, basic telephone Services)	7,542 (1,665)	9,012 (1,997)	265 (48)	57,243 (12,601)	7%
4.	Computer Software and Hardware	3,551 (780)	3,804 (796)	1,337 (251)	51,495 (9,775)	6%
5.	Drugs and Pharmaceuticals	961 (209)	14,605 (3,232)	3,067 (580)	45,935 (9,775)	5%

* Top Five Sectors.

Source: 'Fact sheet on Foreign Direct Investment (FDI)', Department of Industry Policy and Promotion, Ministry of Commerce and Industry, GOI, Available at www.dipp.nic.in

The corporate and the democratic, the two contending forces, who do not have identical needs and interests, claim stake over the process of planning, development and remaking of the city. Urban remaking appears to the respective groups with altogether different meaning. As Nair observes:

> On the one hand are the newly renovated citizens, who are amply aided by a technocratic vision of change offered by the leaders of the New Economy. On the other hand are those for whom, democracy has come to have a different meaning in the urban setting (Nair, 2006: 143).

The thrust on development of car-centric infrastructure in lieu of pedestrian infrastructure in cities may well illustrate the situation. Reports are available to suggest that more than 70 per cent of the investments have been made in car-centric infrastructure including flyovers and road widening across India overlooking the actual travel need of the commuters. In Delhi, 'cars and two-wheelers occupy 90 per cent of the road space but meet less than 20 per cent of the travel demand'. The available comparable data with respect to Kolkata indicate, while flyovers dominated JNNURM Urban Infrastructure funding in Kolkata Metropolitan Area and as much as 73 per cent of the project cost, development of pedestrian and bicycle infrastructure barely received project support. In fact, active policies are often followed to restrict bicycle usage in the city. Cars and two-wheelers occupy the maximum road space but carry just about 12 per cent of the daily trips in Kolkata. The city is being designed for car owners without paying heed to the travel needs of the majority using public transport and walking. The demand for more space for cycles and cycle rickshaws goes unheard (Centre for Science and Environment, 2011). Non-motorized transport (such as bicycles, pedal rickshaws), despite its undeniable advantages vis-à-vis motorized transport, suffer from policy neglect. Urban planning in many cities has no provision for dedicated tracks for the non-motorized mode of transport. In Bengaluru, signal-free corridors, monster flyovers, high-speed toll-ways are the priorities of the civic agencies which even keep the footpaths poorly maintained. The pedestrians find their safety deliberately and systematically compromised. The 'misplaced' priorities of the civic agencies for more and more motorized space survive with costs to the pedestrians and the urban poor in particular (Kappan, 2015).

The cities are facing problems like air and noise pollution, pervasive traffic jams and a decline in safety of cyclists and pedestrian following galloping increase in motorized mode of transport. Additionally, there is the increased burden of expense associated with transportation for the urban poor. The growing expense of transportation results in lower mobility amongst the poor with adverse impacts on their livelihood prospects. Increased expense on travel also limits access to education of dependents. The cities are witnessing a substantial increase in privately-owned vehicle population. A study on six metropolitan cities in India suggests that compared to growth in population, the number of registered vehicles has increased manifold. On an average, between 1981 and 2001, while the population increased 1.89 times, the number of registered vehicles went up 7.75 times during the same period in these cities. The growth in vehicle population has been found to be inversely related to availability of mass transport system in cities without good mass transit systems, like Delhi, Chennai, Hyderabad and Bangalore have a higher growth rate in vehicular population as compared to those with mass transit systems (Aggarwal, 2006; 107). This growth has been largely driven by the growth in the number of two-wheelers. The point that we wish to make here is that the growth in privately-owned motorized mode of transport has led to a decline in the overall use of public transport. The urban poor are still dependent on public transport for mobility either for employment or education. For a variety of reasons, the use of non-motorized mode of transport is on the decline particularly in major cities. A majority of the lower-income population cannot afford private modes of transportation. But the share of public transport vehicles in the total vehicle fleet in India has been declining. Whereas the share of buses in the total motor vehicle fleet was 11 per cent in 1951; it came down to only 1.1 per cent in 2001 (Aggarwal, 2006: 108). The urban transport plans need to take into account the affordability and accessibility needs of the poor, as well.

John Ruskin, the renowned English art critic of the nineteenth century, wrote on various subjects ranging from geology to architecture to literature to political economy. Ruskin once remarked: 'The measure of any great civilization is its cities and a measure of a city's greatness is to be found in the quality of its public spaces, its parks and squares'. The Greek *agora*, is regarded by many as the quintessential public space. The Greek *agora (ah-go-rah)* was basically a place where the people of the town would assemble and where the ceremonies and spectacles would be performed. Though various forms of public spaces have evolved over time, the main character of public spaces has always been the people, everywhere. Be it Greek *agora*, or its contemporary variant, Tiananmen Square of Beijing or, National Mall of Washington DC or, *maidan* of Kolkata.

Public space became a new object of discourse in late nineteenth century colonial India. Public space had no prior history in Indian cities. Prior to this period, Indian cities had physical spaces shared by common people, accessible to all or at least, most of the residents of the city. By naming certain properties and spaces public, drafting rules governing what activities would take place there and enforcing those rules through new urban institutions, the colonial India created both a concept and a corporeal substance – a public space (Glover, 2012: 212).

The urban space has become the site of critical contest. The cities, undergoing redevelopment, witness a spate of real estate activities, fierce battle for gaining control over the urban space to redevelop it for more 'productive' use through elimination/displacement of the 'barriers to urban redevelopment'. A new form of governance that 'integrates state and corporate interests and through the application of money power' has been emerging to ensure 'disbursement of the surplus through the state apparatus favours corporate capital and the upper classes in shaping the urban process' (Harvey, 2008: 38).

The urban space has been conspicuously changing, everywhere. Urban remaking tends to eliminate particular communities and their associated ways of life. 'Regeneration can be indiscriminate in its eradication; places that are valued, rituals and events that are enacted simply disappear. Established communities, everyday rituals, practices of hanging out and making business will be required to make way for new versions of progress' (Carter, 1985: Preface).

Nair's observations, with respect to changing city-space in Bengaluru, the e-city of India and with a proven record of rapid economic growth in recent times, deserve attention. Nair notes:

> The city of Bangalore was once liberally dotted with tanks .... The demand for real estate today has eclipsed all other concerns and the battle for tank beds continues .... The tank beds once considered, open or waste land, fit for occupation for the poor, is the most contested site in Bangalore today. The growing middle class thirst for sites has consumed farmland and village, within and beyond corporation limits, displacing thousands from market-gardening communities and transforming the urban fabric .... At the same time, the need for globalized spaces – five star hotels, golf courses or tech parks which conform to international standards – takes uneasy precedence over the democratic demand of the poor or underprivileged for water, housing, public transport' (Nair, 2000).[2]

A recent study on Rajarhat or New Town, an emerging township 'beyond Kolkata', very well allows one to understand how the new urban centres are being built disrupting livelihood and environment. 'Rajarhat is a surface', as Samaddar puts it:

> made of filled-in ponds, other water bodies, pilfered and acquired what was previously tilled land, vegetable gardens and farms, wetlands, small villages and hamlets .... The farmers, fishermen, vegetable growers and sellers, boatmen, and agricultural labour now robbed of livelihood all roam around these marginal places, if they are not already serving the new comers of Rajarhat with domestic labour, transportation, vegetable supply, or serving tea and sundry Tiffin food (Samaddar, 2011).

'Urban village' very often forms part of metropolitan cities in India. The 'urban village' of the city comes into being when the surrounding agricultural and farm lands, often the principal source of livelihood of many, are sold by the owners or taken away by the state for the purpose of development of 'New Town'. A good example of urban village is the *Kotukbandh Gaon* of Kharghar node in Navi Mumbai or the *Vashi Gaon* of Navi Mumbai (Chatterjee, 2014). One of the stated objectives of the New Bombay Development Plan had been to enable the 'urban villagers' to adapt to the new urban setting and to actively participate in its economic and social life. There were promises of alternative employment and rehabilitation. Little of those promises were implemented. Chatterjee (2014) notes:

> With the start of development of the New Bombay Area, the large majority of local people lost their land, their jobs and their incomes. ... The situation had been very difficult for people those who did not have any land and were not considered as Project Affected People. The landless households did not get any compensation or benefits. Yet, most of these people lost their jobs and incomes and therefore have been more affected than the formal PAPs. The groups which have been most affected are poor agricultural labourers, tribals and fishermen in the area who suffered from these developments.

The malls are emerging as the new variant of urban social space as the traditional urban social spaces have either disappeared or their pristine glories have been lost. The number of malls has been increasing steadily. Many of the upcoming malls will require share of urban space larger than before.[3] The steady inflow of investment in Information and Communication Technology sector and Real Estate sector has induced conspicuous changes particularly in those urban centres where the ICT-based companies are concentrated. The physical appearances of the shopping malls 'may look similar to traditional public space, but in reality, they are greatly restrictive in terms of affordability, accessibility and social meaning'. The unique element of 'publicness' of public space is being increasingly contested in neo-liberal framework of urban development.

The visibility of the cities has been changing with the introduction of new forms of architecture. A new promising urban middle class of professionals has been emerging. This emerging class of urban professionals, accustomed to work 24x7 in a globalized space mainly for the global companies, to live in a self-contained apartment or in a gated residential enclave, to shop in Malls, to use the branded products, tends to develop a distinct lifestyle and world-view. They perform to the sustenance of the 'new-age economy'. They are the 'winners' of the new global economic order. As Bhattacharya and Sanyal put it:

> In Indian cities, a 'new' class of workers, which has been the result of the cities inserting themselves into the hegemonic sectors of the global economy, has increasingly asserted its demands for an aestheticised urban space. The urban elite in many Indian cities, in their aspiration to be located on the map of global economy, are

> pushing through urban transformations as preconditions for entry to the hegemonic sectors of global economy (Bhattacharya and Sanyal, 2011: 41)

The 'new' Indian middle class, 'marked by changing attitudes, consumption pattern and life-style' is engaged, in collaboration with the state, in 'spatial purification' by way of gradually displacing the socially and economically marginalized groups from the urban space. Restructuring of urban space in liberalizing India forms part of wider process of global restructuring under changing social conditions (Fernandes, 2004).

Some urban centres in India are aligned more with the global economy than the national economy. And, by virtue of their strong linkage with the global market, these urban centres have become successful not only in attracting global capital but also in achieving significant economic growth in recent years (Kundu, 2007). The 'meteoric' rise of Bengaluru, is a case in point. Bengaluru, among few other cities in India, is 'linked more with the US and Europe for its economic activities than its immediate surroundings' (Mohan and Dasgupta, 2005: 220). Bengaluru has been successful in ensuring both 'internationalization of trade' and 'internationalization of capital', the two indicators of integration with the global economy (Narayan, 2010: 5). The fruits of economic growth, not being evenly distributed, are leading to uneasy social and economic disparities. As Dittrich depicts the situation in Bengaluru:

> The meteoric rise of Bengaluru ... produce profound changes in the metropolitan social map, creating aggravating disparities and a highly fragmented and polarized urban society .... While a relatively tiny stratum of the urban affluent elite takes benefits from these transformations, the urban poor are further marginalized (Dittrich, 2007: 57).

Steady efforts towards 'internationalization' of the cities leads to steep rise in cost of living. The urban middle class, particularly those dependent on 'old-age economy', is being gradually priced out to the city-fringes/suburbs, the low-cost residential areas where provision for basic facilities are inadequately available. The low-income and the urban poor are being pushed to settle 'far away from the urban labour markets where they make their living'. The 'right to city' is gradually becoming a privilege of a small segment of 'political and economic elite who are in a position to shape cities after their own desires' (Harvey, 2008: 38). On the other hand, the city-fringes/suburbs are witnessing tremendous but unplanned growth. Given the increasing demand for housing, the developers/builders do not find it much difficult to sell a flat built on small plots of land in a narrow lane in city-fringes/suburbs. While the cities are shrinking, the suburbs are growing.

A recent report on size of population in some metros indicates that population in Mumbai, Kolkata and two inner districts of Delhi declined, while Hyderabad and Chennai experienced only a small increase. But surrounding regions of these cities showed phenomenal growth. For instance, Kolkata's population dipped by 2 per cent while population in the surrounding north and south 24 parganas, Hooghly and Howrah districts have all increased by 10 per cent to nearly 20 per cent. Again, two of Delhi's nine districts showed a decline in population between 2001 and 2011 Censuses – New Delhi and Central Delhi. Also, the population of four adjacent districts of Delhi, Gurgaon (now Gurugram), Ghaziabad and Gautam Budh Nagar (Noida) in UP have exploded. Gurgaon (now Gurugram) leads with an increase of 73 per cent in a decade, while Noida grew about 50 per cent and Ghaziabad about 41 per cent. Mumbai City district saw a population dip of about 8 per cent between 2001 and 2011. But Thane grew at 36 per cent and Raigarh district by 19 per cent. Chennai grew by about 7 per cent but Thiruvallur by 35 per cent and Kancheepuram by 40 per cent (*TOI*, 22 June 2014).

In fact, the cities and the mega cities in particular are witnessing, as Kundu defines it, 'degenerative peripheralization'. Kundu (2011) argues:

> Some of India's major cities are experiencing 'degenerative peripheralization' – where the people are driven out by the high cost of living and the scarcity of jobs that pay a decent wage to live in ad hoc settlements on the periphery of metropolitan areas. In those peripheral settlements, people have lost the advantages of both urban and rural life. Big cities are losing the poor because they can't afford to live there ... We are sanitizing our cities. Sanitization means making the environment clean, ... clearing the slums, pushing out the low-income colonies. And in the process, cities miss out on any opportunity to transform the urban poor into drivers of growth and development and instead perceive illiterate, unskilled workers only as liabilities to health, hygiene and law and order. (Kundu, 2011: 78)

Baviskar's critical exploration of the situation in metropolitan Delhi indicates how the 'bourgeois dream of remaking the city' deny the urban poor the right to city (Baviskar, 2003: 93). The anti-poor spatial restructuring in Delhi between 2004 and the beginning of the Commonwealth Games 'was a move to present a sanitized version of Delhi to the visitors' (Ramkrishnan, 2013: 102). More than 5,00,000 families lost their homes from Yamuna Pushta along the river Yamuna in Delhi to make way for 'elite and high-income housing, sports facilities, new roads improving accessibility of automobiles, etc.' (Kumar, 2014: 19).

'Gentrification' (refers to a process by which the low-income households of a locality are displaced by high-income households assuming movement of capital and people resulting in physical, social and economic change) has evolved into a crucial urban strategy across societies wherein the city authority acts in consort with private capital (Smith, 2002). Even where gentrification per se is limited, Smith adds that 'the mobilization of urban real-estate markets as vehicles of capital accumulation is ubiquitous'. A recent cross-cultural study (Mumbai and London) demonstrates how the position of anti-gentrification groups have been weakened, primacy of global capital in setting political agendas has been emphasized and a variety of strategies to attract property investment have been evolved by the political and economic elites, often in tandem, in both situations (Harris, 2008). The landed asset possessed by the closed and the 'sick' factory units, located within the statutory limit of the city or its adjacent areas are the prime target of the real estate sector for more productive use. The South City Mall (Kolkata) is a case in point (Mukherjee, 2011).

The South City Mall, a colossal and possibly the largest of its kind in eastern India, was constructed by the Merlin Group on the land of a closed factory. The Mall assured an aspirational lifestyle and opportunities for gratification of desires 'ignoring livelihood, dismantling structures and destroying a good portion of a huge water body'. As one travels through the stretch from Jadavpur to Garia (both places located in Kolkata South), one notices a row of closed factory units and 'these have either already become or are in the process of becoming housing complexes with shopping malls' (Mukherjee, 2011: 16). Or, as one undertakes a short trip of less than an hour by rail from Sealdah to Naihati, one may also notice a row of closed factory units with dilapidated structures covered with bushes awaiting buyers. Construction is in progress on some of these sites. The phenomenon of gentrification needs to be understood in wider context as part of global strategy for capitalist expansion under changing social conditions.

Urban Remaking II

The rural land is being transformed into urban space often through 'capturing land from the low income population that may have lived there for many years'. There is often coercive intervention of the 'developmental' state. The 'developmental' state mediates – apparently in the name of industrial development – to facilitate the process of capital accumulation. The state mediates to make the key elements of production (and chiefly land) available to capital. Rajarhat or the New Town witnessed a 'paradoxical combination of neo-liberal and primitive modes of capital accumulation' (Samaddar, 2013). The intervention of the coercive state to allow capital 'to overcome the barriers to accumulation' generates debate over the process of acquisition of land for industrial development/Special Economic Zone (SEZ) and the compensation and rehabilitation package for the displaced. Scholastic disagreement persists about the beneficial implications of SEZs. SEZ remains a contentious issue. It is best put in some detail.

EPZ and SEZ

The Export Processing Zone (EPZ) and the Special Economic Zone (SEZ) are the two dominant economic zones found across economies. EPZ, a relatively old model, is basically an export-based growth strategy. EPZs are 'special enclaves, separated from Domestic Tariff Area by fiscal barriers and are intended to provide an internationally competitive duty-free environment for export production at low cost' (Aggarwal, 2004: 3). The World Bank (1981) defines an EPZ as 'a clearly delineated industrial estate, which constitutes a free trade enclave in the customs and trade regime of a country and where foreign manufacturing firms producing mainly for export benefit from a certain number of fiscal and financial incentives' (Lakshmanan, 2009). Since the early 1960s, the developing economies have greatly relied upon the EPZ model. This model has been appreciated for significant contribution to export-driven growth in the Asian region. China, encouraged by the experiences of EPZs in Asia, relied upon its open-door policy further, to create the SEZs between late 1970s and early 1980s 'aiming not only at export-oriented industrialization but also the promotion of national development and as laboratories for the on-going economic reform' (Amirahamadi and Wu, 1995: 828). To distinguish between an EPZ and an SEZ, while an EPZ is just an industrial enclave, an SEZ 'is almost a self-contained area with high class infrastructure for commercial operations as well as residential inhabitation' (Lakshmanan, 2009). The SEZs are ordinarily established to achieve either or more of the following objectives (FIAS, 2008):

1. To attract foreign direct investment
2. To alleviate large-scale unemployment
3. To facilitate wider economic reform strategy
4. To facilitate experiment with new policies and approaches

The traditional EPZ model is being gradually replaced by the SEZ model across societies. The traditional EPZ model has been successful in 'attracting investment and creating employment in the short term but have failed to remain sustainable when the labour costs have risen or when preferential trade access no longer offers a sufficient advantage' (Farole and Akinci, 2011: 4). The changing global trade and investment environment is no longer supportive to the traditional EPZ model, either. The phenomenal increase in number of SEZs in almost all regions, with concentration in developing economies, obviously suggests that the attraction of the policy makers for SEZs as an instrument of trade, investment, industrial and spatial policy has been increasingly growing. According to one estimate of the International Labour Organization, while there were 176 Zones in 47 countries in 1986, the number has increased to 3,500 Zones in 130 countries in 2005 (Table 9).

EPZ and SEZ in India

In 1965, Asia's first Export Processing Zone (EPZ) was set up in Kandla. Santacruz EPZ came up in 1973. Later, in the late 1980s, five more EPZs were set up. Surat EPZ started operation towards the end of 1990s. Nineteen (19) Zones were established/notified prior to the enactment of the SEZ Act 2005. The major objectives of the EPZs in India was not clear until it was clarified in a report of the Comptroller and Auditor General of India that 'the EPZs were meant for earning of foreign exchange, develop export-oriented industries, stimulate investment and generate employment opportunities ...' (Aggarwal, 2004: 2). How did these EPZs fare?

The available reports on the performance of the EPZs, measured in terms of export of goods and services, earning of foreign exchange and generation of employment (i.e.; the three major objectives for which the EPZs had been established), suggest that the performance of the EPZs was impressive in absolute terms on all these segments. Between 1966 and 2002, EPZ exports increased from less than ₹ 1 million to over ₹ 97,727 million. Over the same period, total employment increased from only 70 to around 89,000 and net foreign exchange earnings increased from ₹ 0.16 million to ₹ 43,195 million (Aggarwal, 2004: 9).

The performance of the EPZs in India was, however, not consistent. The EPZs fared well during the initial years and thereafter the rate of growth started declining. Available authoritative data on the average annual export growth rate points to the fact that while the average annual export growth rate was over 77 per cent between 1966 and 1980, it came down to 42.3 per cent in the 1980s and touched the level as low as 7 per cent between 2001 and 2003 (Table 10). In so far as the issue of generation of employment in EPZs was concerned, the available authoritative data indicate a similar trend. The data, showing the trend in employment suggest, opportunities for employment in EPZs increased substantially from 70 to 89,000 between 1966 and 2002 (Table 11).

Table 9

Estimate of the Development of Export Processing Zones

Years	*1975*	*1986*	*1997*	*2002*	*2006*
Number of countries with EPZs	25	47	93	116	130
Number of EPZs or similar types of zones	79	176	845	3,000	3,500
Employment (millions)	NA	NA	22.5	43	66
–of which China	NA	NA	18	30	40
–of which other countries with figures available	0.8	1.9	4.5	13	26

Source: Boyenge, Jean-Pierre Singa (2007): 'ILO database on export processing Zones', Working Paper (251), International Labour Organization, Geneva, p. 1.

Table 10

Export Performance of EPZs in India (1966–2002)
(₹ in Million)

	Average Annual Total Exports	*Average Annual Growth Rate in Export*
1966–1970	03.261	94.6502
1971–1975	17.358	58.3438
1976–1980	186.766	79.2688
1966–1980 Average	69.1	77.42
1981–1985	2,317.24	57.5374
1986–1990	5,829.1	27.113
1981–1990 Average	4,073.1	42.3
1991–1995	20,848.74	27.1862
1996–2000	59,184.79	21.68
1991–2000 Average	40,017	24.4
2001–2003	93,251.75	7.32
2001–2003 Average	93,251.75	7.32

Source: Ministry of Commerce, GOI (as cited in Aggarwal, 2004: 12)

Table 11

Growth in Employment in EPZs (1966–2002)

Year	*Total Employment (Number)*	*Average EPZ Employment (Number)*	*Average Employment Growth Rate between Two Years (%)*
1966	70	70	
1970	450	450	50.2
1975	1,450	725	41.9
1980	6,000	3,000	34.2
1985	16,200	4,050	22.6
1990	35,205	5,868	16.9
1995	61,431	10,239	11.9
2000	81,371	11,624	6.2
2002	88,977	12,711	5.2

Source: Ministry of Commerce, GOI (as cited in Aggarwal, 2004: 13).

However, the average annual growth rate in employment declined steadily, over the years. Also, this was true to earning in foreign exchange. It was 'while the value of net foreign exchange in absolute terms increased phenomenally after the mid 1980s, the rate at which it grew remained stagnant and in fact started declining after 1998' (Aggarwal, 2004: 18).

In India, the policy to create SEZ was first announced in April 2000 (EXIM Policy). Between 2000 and 2003, all EPZs were formally notified as SEZs. Until the SEZ Act, 2005, initiated significant changes, the basic framework was, however, kept unaltered. The SEZ Act (2005) was passed by the Parliament in May 2005 to demonstrate 'the government's commitment to a stable SEZ regime' necessary to 'instill confidence in investors'. The SEZ Act (2005), supported by SEZ Rules, came into effect in 2006 (February) limiting the role of the central government with respect to SEZs. The private sector developers were entrusted with the responsibility 'to fund and manage the entire project on a commercial basis' (Menon and Mitra, 2009: 12). The SEZ Act (2005), since its passage, invited both appreciation and voice of concern. The voice of concern, rose against certain provisions of the SEZ Act of 2005, led to the enactment of a protective legislation in 2013. The voices of concern against certain provisions of the said Act led to the enactment of the Right to Fair Compensation and Transparency in Land Acquisition, Rehabilitation and Resettlement Act 2013, to ensure:

> A humane, participative, informed and transparent process for land acquisition for industrialization, development of essential infrastructural facilities and urbanization ... to provide just and fair compensation to the affected families ... make adequate provisions for their rehabilitation and resettlement ... leading to an improvement in their post-acquisition social and economic status (Gazette of India, 2013: 1).

SEZ: Major Objectives

The SEZ Act (2005) had been enacted with the following major objectives:

1. Generation of additional economic activities
2. Promotion of exports of goods and services
3. Promotion of investment from domestic and foreign sources
4. Creation of employment opportunities

5. Development of infrastructural facilities

The SEZ Act (2005) had been designed to attract investment (domestic as well as foreign) to promote exports of goods and services, to develop infrastructure and to create employment opportunities. These objectives indicate India's preference for an export-oriented developmental strategy as pursued by many developing economies under changing social conditions.

As per the SEZ Act (2005), a SEZ may be established either jointly or severally by the central government; state government or any person for manufacturing of goods or rendering services or both or as a Free trade and Warehousing Zone. The SEZ Act (2005) envisages details related to approval and authorization to developer, guidelines for notifying SEZ, exemption from taxes, duties and cess, procedure of approval, single window clearance and special fiscal provisions for SEZ and such other matters (SEZ Act, 2005). The SEZ units and developer are offered incentives and facilities.

The incentives and facilities extended to the units include:

1. Duty free import/domestic procurement of goods for development, operation and maintenance of SEZ units.
2. 100 per cent Income Tax exemption on export income for SEZ units for first 5 years, 50 per cent for next 5 years thereafter and 50 per cent of the ploughed back export profit for next 5 years.
3. Exemption from minimum alternate tax.
4. External commercial borrowing by SEZ units up to US $ 500 million in a year without any maturity restriction through recognized banking channels.
5. Exemption from Central Sales Tax.
6. Exemption from Service Tax.
7. Single window clearance for central and state level approvals.
8. Exemption from state sales tax and other levies as extended by the respective state governments.

The major incentives and facilities available to SEZ developers include:

1. Exemption from customs/excise duties for development of SEZs for authorized operations approved by the Board of Approval.

2. Income Tax exemption on income derived from the business of development of the SEZ in a block of 10 years in 15 years.
3. Exemption from minimum alternate tax.
4. Exemption from dividend distribution tax.
5. Exemption from Central Sales.
6. Exemption from Service Tax. (www.sezindia.nic.in)

Minimum Area Requirement for SEZ

The SEZ Act, 2005, stipulates minimum land area requirement for setting up SEZ (SEZ Rules, 2006). The area is notified as SEZ upon formal consent of the Board of Approval and the report of the concerned Development Commissioner certifying the contiguity and vacancy of the area. The minimum area requirement for different categories of SEZ is shown here-in-below (Box 1):

BOX 1

Minimum Area Requirement for SEZ (Category-wise)

SEZ Category	Minimum Area (in hectares)
Multi Sector SEZ	1,000
Sector Specific SEZ	100
FTWZ (Free Trade Warehousing Zone)	40
IT/ITES/Handicrafts SEZ/Bio-technology/ Non-Conventional Energy/Gems and Jewellery Sector	10

Amendment was intended at permitting optimum utilization of land by the existing SEZs. The Amendment permits setting up of various categories of SEZ with minimum land area requirement as stated below (Box 2):

Box: 2

Revised Area Requirement for SEZ

SEZ Category	Minimum Area (in hectares)
Multi Sector SEZ	500
Sector Specific SEZ	50
IT/ITES SEZ	No minimum land area but minimum built-up area
Agro-based SEZ New sector introduced with minimum land area req.	10

The minimum land requirement criterion of 10 hectares for setting up IT/ITES SEZ, as it was originally envisaged, has been dispensed with. As per the SEZ (Amendment) Rules, 2013, the IT/ITES SEZ will now have to conform to minimum built-up area requirement in place of minimum land area requirement. The requirement of minimum built up area varies depending upon the category of cities with 1 lakh sq. mt. for the seven cities viz. Mumbai, Delhi (NCR), Hyderabad, Chennai, Pune, Bangalore and Kolkata. For the category B cities, 50,000 sq. mt. norm will be applicable. For the remaining cities/locations, the minimum built up area requirement will be 25,000 sq. mt. Further, the SEZ (Amendment) Rules, 2013, envisages introduction of a new sector viz.; agro-based food processing sector. A sector-specific SEZ in this sector will require a minimum land area requirement of 10 hectares.

Growth of SEZs

In India, there has been phenomenal growth in number of SEZs since the enactment of the SEZ Act (2005). As it has already been stated, there were only 19 SEZs prior to the enactment of the SEZ Act 2005. The number of SEZs, which have been granted formal approval under the SEZ Act (2005), is 574. The number of notified SEZs is 391. The number of operational SEZs is 175. This is inclusive of seven SEZs established by the central government and 12 State/Private Sector SEZs established prior to the enactment of the SEZ Act, 2005 (Table 12). A state-wise distribution of the SEZs (approved/in principle approved/notified) under the SEZ Act, 2005, reveals that the number of SEZs with formal approval is highest in Andhra Pradesh (109) followed by Maharashtra (102), Tamil Nadu (67) and Karnataka (61) and Gujarat (43). Maharashtra occupies the top position in terms of in-principle approved SEZs (16). The number of notified SEZs is highest in Andhra Pradesh (78) followed by Maharashtra (65) and Tamil Nadu (53). Table 13 relates to state-wise distribution of land area for approved SEZs. It is evident, while total land area notified for approved 576 SEZs is 61,545 hectares, the three states, to be specific, Gujarat, Andhra Pradesh and Maharashtra occupy more than 67 per cent of total land area. Table 14 provides data with respect to Zone-wise land use by the notified SEZs. Evidently, a total land area of 47,803.77 hectares was notified for 408 notified SEZs under seven Zones. Of the total notified land area of 47,803.77 for 408 notified SEZs,

21,313.03 hectares of land area is vacant. A sector-wise distribution of operational SEZs reveals dominance of IT/ITES sector over other sectors (Table 15).

SEZ in India: Major Trends

The major trends, as revealed through the data on SEZs presented above, may be mentioned as follows:

First, the number of operational SEZs is limited. Of the 574 SEZs, approved under the SEZ Act, 2005, 391 SEZs have been notified. The number of operational SEZs is only 175 (including 19 SEZs which were established prior to the enactment of the SEZ Act, 2005) indicating that less than one-third (30.14) of the approved SEZs is only operational (Table 12).

Second, there is geographical concentration of SEZs in India. As evident from state-wise distribution of approved SEZs, five states viz.; Andhra Pradesh, Maharashtra, Tamil Nadu, Karnataka and Gujarat dominate. More than 66 per cent of approved SEZs are located in these five states. Again, more than 76% of operational SEZs are also located in these five states (Table 12). Regional disparity in terms of location of SEZs persists.

Table 12

State-Wise Distribution of Approved/Notified/Exporting SEZs in India

State-Wise Distribution of Approved SEZs (As on 05.12.2013)

State	*Formal Approvals*	*Notified SEZs*	*Operational (Exporting) SEZs*
Andhra Pradesh	109	78	40
Chandigarh	2	2	2
Chhattisgarh	2	1	1
Delhi	3	0	0
Dadra & Nagar Haveli	2	1	0
Goa	7	3	0
Gujarat	43	30	18
Haryana	45	34	5
Jharkhand	1	1	0

Cont'd...

...Cont'd

Karnataka	61	40	22
Kerala	29	24	8
Madhya Pradesh	19	9	2
Maharashtra	101	65	20
Manipur	1	0	0
Nagaland	2	2	0
Odisha	10	5	1
Puducherry	1	0	0
Punjab	8	2	2
Rajasthan	10	10	5
Tamil Nadu	67	53	34
Uttar Pradesh	31	21	9
Uttarakhand	2	1	0
West Bengal	18	9	6
Grand Total	574	391	175

Source: Press Information Bureau, GOI, (Ministry of Commerce and Industry, 13 December 2013), http://pib.nic.in/newsite/PrintRelease.aspx?relid=101162

Table 13

State-Wise Distribution of Land Area for SEZ

S. No.	*State/UTs*	*Total Area of Formal Approvals (in hectares)*
1.	Andhra Pradesh	15,374.81
2.	Chandigarh	58.46
3.	Chhattisgarh	112.05
4.	Delhi	33.25
5.	Dadra & Nagar Haveli	22.46
6.	Goa	369.99
7.	Gujarat	14,780.66
8.	Haryana	1,787.37
9.	Jharkhand	36.42
10.	Karnataka	2,834.55

Cont'd...

...Cont'd

11.	Kerala	1,143.28
12.	Madhya Pradesh	868.41
13.	Maharashtra	11,313.99
14.	Manipur	10.85
15.	Nagaland	340.70
16.	Orissa	2,029.26
17.	Pondicherry	346.00
18.	Punjab	209.25
19.	Rajasthan	633.42
20.	Tamil Nadu	7,725.35
21.	Uttar Pradesh	453.54
22.	Uttarakhand	647.02
23.	West Bengal	413.66
	Total	61,545

Source: Press Information Bureau, GOI, (Ministry of Commerce and Industry, 13 December 2013), http://pib.nic.in/newsite/PrintRelease.aspx?relid=101162

Table 14

*Zone-Wise Distribution of Land Area (Notified/Utilized/Vacant)**

(Area in Hectares)

Name of Zone	*Number SEZs of Notified*	*Total Notified Area*	*Total Area Utilized*	*Total Area Vacant*
Cochin SEZ	65	3,192.49	1,298.04	1,534.00
Madras SEZ	58	5,380.42	2,202.64	2,738.56
Noida SEZ	82	4,671.53	671.50	1,288.08
Vishakhapatnam SEZ	80	12,168.68	4,172.01	4,425.85
Kandla SEZ	33	12,889.99	6,880.26	5,172.89
Falta SEZ	20	1,264.64	571.13	774.25
SEEPZ SEZ Mumbai	70	8,236.02	1,893.48	5,376.40
Total	408	47,803.77	17,689.06	21,310.03

* as on 23.01.2014

Source: www.sezindia.nic.in

Table 15

Sector-Wise Distribution of Approved SEZs (As on 30.4.2014)

Sectors	*Formal Approvals*	*In-principle Approvals*	*Notified SEZ s*	*Exporting SEZs (Central Govt+ State Govt./Pvt. SEZs+ notified SEZs under the SEZ Act, 2005*
Agro	6	2	5	0
Airport-based multi-product	4	0	0	0
Auto and related	2	1	1	1
Aviation/Aerospace/Copper/ Animation and Gaming	5	1	6	5
Beach and mineral/metals	3	0	3	0
Bio-tech	30	0	19	2
Building products/mal/transport equipment/material	2	2	2	2
Electronic prod/industries	3	0	3	1
Engineering	17	1	13	11
Food Processing	5	0	4	4
Footwear/Leather	6	0	5	3
FTWZ	13	5	7	3
Gems and Jewellery	13	3	6	3
Granite processing industries and other allied machinery/manufacturing	2	0	1	0
Handicrafts and Carpets	5	0	3	3
IT/ITES/Electronic Hardware/Semiconductor	348	1	238	102
Metal/Stain Steel/Alum/Foundary	8	2	5	0
Light Engineering/Metallurgical Engineering/Automotive Components	1	0	0	0

Cont'd...

...Cont'd

Multi-Product	24	13	16	19
Multi-Services/Services	11	3	8	2
Non-Conventional Energy	6	0	4	2
Petrochemicals and petrol/oil and gas	4	1	2	1
Pharma/Chemicals	22	2	20	11
Plastic/Processing	0	2	0	0
Port-based multi-product	7	2	2	1
Power/Alternate Energy/Solar	3	1	3	3
Textiles/Apparel/Wool	14	1	11	6
Writing and printing paper mills	2	0	1	0
Grand Total	566	43	388	185

Source: http://www.sezindia.nic.in/writereaddata/pdf/Sector-wise%20distribution-SEZ.pdf

Third, as evident from the state-wise distribution of land area for SEZs, three states, to be specific, Gujarat, Andhra Pradesh and Maharashtra occupy more than 67 per cent of total land area (Table 13).

Fourth, data are available to suggest that the SEZs do not always make use of total notified land area. A zone-wise distribution of land area reveals that the proportion of land area that remains vacant is greater than that of land area utilized by the Notified SEZs (Table 14).

Fifth, a sector-wise distribution of approved SEZs shows numerical domination of IT/ITES sector-specific SEZ over other sectors including the multi-product/services sector SEZs. Out of 173 operational SEZs, 92 are IT/ITES SEZs and only 20 are multi-product/services SEZs (Table 15).

Sixth, the SEZs are smaller in size. As evident from sector-wise distribution of Operational SEZs (Table 8), more than 53 per cent of SEZs are IT/ITES sector-specific SEZs which required minimum land area of 10 hectares (prior to passage of the SEZ (Amendment) Rules 2013).

Seventh, the SEZs in India are urban-centric. Reports on geographical location of the SEZs suggest that the SEZs are located in close proximity to cities/urban agglomerates. While prime agricultural land in or around cities/urban agglomerates is preferred for SEZs, the unutilized part of land area, notified for industrial activities, is eventually utilized for real estate activities.

Finally, there is no reason to believe that land area of SEZ and employment is positively related. While the operational SEZs in Andhra Pradesh and Gujarat occupy about 49 per cent of total land area of 61,545 hectares, the operational SEZs in these two states generate only 17.82 per cent of total employment generated by SEZs in India. The operational SEZs in Maharashtra, Tamil Nadu and Karnataka together, on the other hand, occupy 35.54 per cent of total land area but generate 62.02 per cent of total employment. While Andhra Pradesh and Gujarat occupy the first and second position, respectively, in terms of land area of SEZs, these two states slip to fourth and sixth rank, respectively, when the indicator of employment is taken into account (Table 16).

SEZ in India: Performance

As it has been mentioned earlier, it was thought that the SEZs shall, among others, promote exports, attract investment and generate employment. The performance of the SEZs in these three sectors during 2009–10/2012–13 and the current financial year (2013–14) has been looked into. It is true that SEZs have played a crucial role in promoting exports. However, its role in diversifying exports has been limited. Exports from SEZs have increased in absolute value over the years. The share of SEZ export to total export is not negligible, either (Table 17). It is true that recent trends in exports from SEZs allow us to be optimistic ('measured in terms of total value of exports'). It is also true that 'it is still not comparable to the SEZs in other countries' (Tantri, 2010: 13–14).

The SEZs in India are not comparable to other countries for at least two reasons. These are: first, despite having multi-product base, two sectors viz. gems and jewellery and electronics contribute to about 77 per cent of total conventional exports from SEZs in India; second, owing to changing sectoral composition of SEZ exports, exports remain concentrated in a few countries and USA in particular (Tantri, 2010: 13).

Table 16

Status of States in Terms of Approved and Operational SEZs, Land Area and Employment

Rank	*Status of States (Top 10)*			
	Approved SEZs (Number)	*Operational SEZs (Number)*	*Land Area (in Hectares)*	*Employment (Number)*
1.	Andhra Pradesh (109)	Andhra Pradesh (40)	Andhra Pradesh (15,375)	Maharashtra (2,79,616)
2.	Maharashtra (101)	Tamil Nadu (34)	Gujarat (14,781)	Tamil Nadu (2,62,486)
3.	Tamil Nadu (67)	Karnataka (22)	Maharashtra (11,314)	Karnataka (1,75,348)
4.	Karnataka (61)	Maharashtra (20)	Tamil Nadu (7,725)	Andhra Pradesh (1,49,226)
5.	Haryana (45)	Gujarat (18)	Karnataka (2,835)	Uttar Pradesh (79,215)
6.	Gujarat (43)	Uttar Pradesh (9)	Haryana (1,787)	Gujarat (56,909)
7.	Uttar Pradesh (31)	Kerala (8)	Kerala (1,143)	West Bengal (47,678)
8.	Kerala (29)	West Bengal (6)	Madhya Pradesh (868)	Haryana (44,887)
9.	Madhya Pradesh (19)	Haryana (5)	Uttar Pradesh (647)	Kerala (29,634)
10.	West Bengal (18)	Madhya Pradesh (2)	West Bengal (414)	Madhya Pradesh (10,141)
Top 10 Total	(523)	(164)	(56,889)	(11,35,140)
Share (%) of Total	91 574	94 391	92.43 61,544.75	98 11,56,677

Source: www.sezindia.nic.in

Table 17

Trend in Exports from SEZs in India (in ₹ Crore)

Trend in Exports				
Financial Year	*Total Export in the Country*	*Total SEZ Export*	*Share of SEZ Export of Total Export (%)*	*SEZ Growth Rate over Previous FY(%)*
2008–09	8,40,755	99,689		
2009–10	8,45,534	2,20,711		
2010–11	11,42,922	3,15,867.60	27.64	43.11
2011–12	14,65,959	3,64,477.73	24.86	15.39
2012–13	16,35,261	4,76,159	29.12	31
2013–14	18,92,892	4,94,077	26.10	

Source: Minutes of BoA Meeting (www.sezindia.nic.in); Annual Report (2012–13), Ministry of Commerce, GOI.
http://commerce.nic.in/publications/anualreport_chapter3-2012-13.asp
Press Information Bureau (14 July 2014)
http://pib.nic.in/newsite/PrintRelease.aspx?relid=106479

Table 18

Trend in Investment in SEZs in India

Trend in Investment in SEZ	
Financial Year	*Investment in SEZ (in ₹ Crore)*
2009–10	
2010–11	2,02,809.54
2011–12	2,01,874.76
2012–13	2,38,990.18
2013–14*	2,88,476.98

* April 2013 to December 2013.

Source: Minutes of BoA Meeting (www.sezindia.nic.in).

A review of performance of SEZs, measured in terms of investment and employment, suggest that SEZs are losing their sheen. As evident from Table 18, investments in SEZs in India have slowed down in recent years. The Pre-Budget Economic Survey 2013–14, placed before the Parliament, indicated that 'there are also areas where SEZs are worse off than Domestic Tariff Area

(DTA) units' (Hindu, 2014: 15). It is argued that the imposition of Minimum Alternate Tax (MAT) and Dividend Distribution Tax (DDT) in 2011 is one of the responsible factors for slow-down in investment in SEZs. Again, there is non-applicability of FTA concessions when SEZs sell in DTAs. While lack of opportunities for forward and backward linkages remains a problem in India, many countries have well defined policies for sales made from SEZs to DTA though with certain restrictions.

SEZ contributes to creation of direct and indirect employment opportunities. Also, SEZs create employment opportunities for women. Trend in direct employment in SEZs is shown in Table 19. While bulk of employment (76.06%) has been generated in SEZ units which came up under the SEZ Act (2005), the employment share of SEZ units which were established prior to the passage of the SEZ Act, 2005, is about 24 per cent (Table 20). The cumulative direct employment generated by SEZs appears to be encouraging while it is taken into account that the first SEZ in India (Kandla) started its operation with only 70 workers on roll. The contribution of SEZ to total employment, however, remains insignificant. The share of SEZ of total employment in manufacturing sector, which has all along been rather marginal, could be one major reason as to why SEZs have failed to generate substantial employment. The share of SEZ of total employment in manufacturing sector never exceeded 1.31 per cent between 1961 and 2006 (Table 21).

Table 19

Trend in Employment in SEZs in India

Financial Year	*Employment in SEZs (Number of Persons)**	*Growth over Previous Year (%)*
2009–10	5,03,611	
2010–11	6,76,608	34.35
2011–12	8,44,916	24.87
2012–13	10,74,904	27.22
2013–14	12,83,309	19.39

* Calculated on cumulative basis.

Source: Minutes of BoA Meeting (www.sezindia.nic.in) &
Press Information Bureau (11 July 2014)
http://pib.nic.in/newsite/PrintRelease.aspx?relid=106479

As indicated earlier, the employment-intensive sectors have failed to attract adequate attention of the SEZ developers in India. Boosting exports from the employment-intensive sectors have the additional advantage in that these sectors can create opportunities for employment to a large number of workers and that too, mostly in unorganized sector. Realizing the critical role of manufacturing in earning of foreign exchange through exports as well as generation of employment, the National Manufacturing Policy (NMP) had been announced in 2011 (NMP, 2011).

Table 20

Category-Wise Employment in SEZs in India

Category-Wise Employment in SEZs			
SEZ Category	*Employment Persons as on February 2006*	*Incremental*	*Total Employment Persons as on March 2014*
Central Govt. SEZs	1,22,236	1,07,248	2,29,484
State/Pvt. SEZs set prior to SEZ Act	12,468	65,215	77,683
SEZs Notified under	0	9,76,142	9,76,142 the SEZ Act
Total	1,34,704	11,48,605	12,83,309

Source: www.sezindia.nic.in/writereaddata/pdf/factsheet.pdf

Table 21

Share of SEZ Employment in Manufacturing Employment in India in Selected Years between 1966 and 2006

Year	*SEZ Employment (Number)*	*Share in Manufacturing Employment (%)*
1966	70	–
1973	300	0.01
1980	6,000	0.09
1990	35,205	0.48
1998	77,795	0.91
2000	81,371	1.03
2005	1,00,650	1.05
2006	1,34,704	1.31

Source: Aggarwal, 2007: 18.

The NMP has been designed to raise the share of manufacturing from the current level of 15–16 per cent to 25 per cent of GDP and creation of 100 million jobs by 2022. As it has been elaborated elsewhere,[4] one of the key instruments to catalyse the growth of manufacturing, will be to establish National Investment and Manufacturing Zones across the country. The clusters ('a concentration of manufacturing industry units located within a clearly demarcated area with the land use notified as such by the state government') will be eligible for NIMZ-specific benefits and dispensations as under the National Manufacturing Policy. Later, guidelines have been issued extending benefits/dispensations, except NIMZ-specific benefits/dispensations, for clusters outside National Investment and Manufacturing Zones (NIMZs) under the National Manufacturing Policy (Manufacturing, 2014: 1)

Nevertheless, the ill-educated, the ill-trained and the ill-skilled persons with no prior acquaintance with the formal economy as an earner find an opportunity in the SEZs developed in the locality/neighbouring areas. The otherwise ill-equipped local unemployed population gets absorbed in the labour-intensive sectors after on-the-job training. Viewed from this perspective, SEZs may operate as an instrument in generating employment and alleviating poverty at the local (Aggarwal, 2007: 19).

A better understanding of the situation obviously calls for an examination of the data on direct employment in SEZs in the light of fall in employment in agriculture during the same period. An understanding of net addition to employment in SEZs – though exceedingly important – becomes difficult as adequate and reliable data on loss of employment on land, which have been acquired for the development of SEZs, are scarce. Again, the domination of IT/ITES sector suggests that much of direct employment in SEZs has been generated by this sector and these work-organizations require skilled workforce and at least not those declared surplus labour on land. Evidences are there to suggest that the dispossessed farmers are generally ill-equipped to be engaged in the SEZs requiring skilled manpower. As Levien, based on empirically derived data from Mahindra World City in Rajasthan, observes:

> When large companies enter a rural village, a considerable hope of residents is that they or their kids will receive employment. Indeed, this is often the promise given by the companies and

> governments to convince farmers that they will benefit from having their land acquired .... Consequently, the only jobs that most local people can hope to get in the SEZ are as gardeners, drivers, guards, or cleaners. These jobs are sub-contracted out to various contractors *(takedars)* and are therefore temporary, insecure and low paying, at around less than US$75 per month (less than the income from keeping two buffalo) .... Only 14 per cent of the sample received some employment in the SEZ, all of them through contractors (and those who lost land complain that this is only one job when the whole family has become unemployed). The only other opportunity is to do construction labour for US$ 3 per day through even more informal labour contractors .... I did not encounter one person from any of the villages who is directly employed by Mahindra, Infosys or Deutsche Bank (Levien, 2011: 476–77).

For the Polepally Pharmaceutical SEZ in Andhra Pradesh, around 1,150 acres of land was acquired from three adjoining villages viz. Polepally, Gundlagadda Thanda and Muddireddipally. Of these, a total of 693 acres had been acquired from 339 households in Polepally village. Of 339 land losing households, the owners of 'assigned land' (i.e.; those who received land under the land reform programme) were eligible for token compensation (not at the market value). A great majority of those who lost 'assigned land' were from Scheduled Castes, Scheduled Tribes and Backward Communities. The others, the owners of 'acquired land' were eligible for compensation according to market value as assessed by the state. The policy of compensation for acquired land was based on: first, legal status of the land and not of the income accrued from the land; second, compensation is related to loss of land and not loss of livelihood (Rawat et al., 2011: 12). The authors added:

> with the exception of two respondents, no member of the affected families has been provided with vocational training so that they could be engaged in the SEZ on a regular and on-going basis. Many members of these families did work as the daily wage labourer during the construction of pharmaceutical units .... After Granite compound walls were constructed, men from affected families were refused further entry into the Pharma units. Some of their women get daily wage for work as gardener or sweeper or janitor. They are paid ₹ 100 per day (Rawat et al., 2011: 13).

Why has SEZ become a contentious issue? Is it that the SEZ has been a controversial issue because of performance below expectations? It is true that the critics very often point to below expectations economic performance of SEZs compared to huge loss of revenue due to fiscal relaxations extended to the developers and units of SEZs. It is also apprehended that geographical concentration of SEZs is likely to result in 'regional imbalances in terms of development'. However, the available reports on protests against SEZ across the country demonstrate that the process of acquisition of land for SEZs, its consequences for the livelihood of innumerable (including the non-owners of acquired land), dissatisfaction of the land losers over inadequacy of compensation as well as delay in delivery of assured compensation and rehabilitation package against dispossession and displacement and such other issues (e.g.; environmental) have surfaced and have been found to be more crucial in fuelling the debate over SEZ in recent times than the issues like performance of SEZs below expectations or, 'biased tax incentives leading to substantial revenue loss'.

Reports are available to suggest that protests at the local level, confrontation between protesters, the police and the administration were frequent and widespread (West Bengal, Orissa, Maharashtra, Goa). Of reported protests, most notable were the protests against the proposed chemical hub (Salem Group) in Nandigram in West Bengal in March 2007. The violence claimed the lives of 14 villagers. The other was the protest against the steel-sector SEZ in Orissa (POSCO).

The protests of the local communities had at least a couple of immediate impacts. The state governments became more cautious in acquisition of land for SEZ. And, the issues of compensation, rehabilitation and resettlement of the project 'affected families' (land losers as well as livelihood losers) received better attention. The passage of the Right to Fair Compensation and Transparency in Land Acquisition, Rehabilitation and Resettlement Act, 2013, was the outcome of such concern.[5] It needs to be mentioned that the aforesaid Act was not well taken by a good number of states. Some states have demanded a review of the Right to Fair Compensation and Transparency in Land Acquisition, Rehabilitation and Resettlement Act, 2013, as the said Act is feared to be a potential impediment to acquisition of land for industrialization. In fact, the call for changes to 'right to fair compensation and transparency in Land Acquisition, Rehabilitation and Resettlement Act 2013, started with the very title of the law that was said to be unnecessarily long' (*TOI*, 2014). The state of West Bengal alone opposed forcible acquisition of land even for the projects of the state. The industry was not happy with the Act, obviously.

As indicated earlier, the state often deploys coercive power to facilitate the process of capital accumulation by way of making the key elements of production (and land in particular) available to capital for industrial, commercial and residential purposes. The SEZ phenomenon demonstrates that the rural land is being commodified and transformed into urban space with the mediation of state. Capital has become global and more mobile than ever before. As well, capital and state are in greater collaboration in remaking the cities and transforming rural land into urban space for more gainful use than at any previous time (Smith, 2003: xxi).

The intervention, often coercive, of the state to allow capital 'to overcome the barriers to accumulation' generates scholastic disagreement about the very essence of the process of capital accumulation under neo-liberalism. The debate continues, whether or not, the process of 'accumulation by dispossession' is a *'decidedly political'* process through which the state's coercive power is deployed to the advantage of capital (Levien, 2011: 457) rather than a *'primarily economic'* process of 'over-accumulated capital finding new outlets' (Harvey, 2006).[6]

Lefebvre once suggested:

> real estate in a neo-capitalist society functions as a second sector .... This second sector serves as a buffer. It is where capital flows in the event of a depression .... As the principal circuit ... begins to slow down capital shifts to the second sector, real estate. It can even happen that real estate speculation becomes the principal source for the formation of capital, that is, the realization of surplus value. As the percentage of overall surplus value formed and realized by industry begins to decline, the percentage created and realized by real estate speculation and construction increases. The second circuit supplants the first, becomes essential (Lefebvre, 1970: 159).

It is true that the real estate, the second circuit, has not supplanted the 'principal circuit', as yet. It is also true that aggressive promotion of urban real estate sector for 'conquest' of urban space 'has been the central motive force of urban economic expansion' (Smith, 2002: 447).[7]

Perhaps, the basic to city-life is diversity. When urbanization tends to become exclusionary, diversity is threatened. The critical contest over urban space for more productive use and the conflict between notions – corporate and democratic – of urbanization demand social security in this light, also.

That agricultural sector alone can't absorb the problem of unemployment and that other sectors of economy need to be encouraged to grow for generation of employment opportunities are seldom contested. Thus acquisition of rural land for the growth of other sectors may become necessary. In such a situation, the state may act as the facilitator to ensure fair compensation and rehabilitation of the losers of land and livelihood. The state needs to oversee, for the welfare of the community around, utilization of the acquired land for the purpose originally pledged within a reasonable period.

Notes

1. The term 'real estate' refers to 'the land, including the air above it and the ground below it, and any building or structures on it'. The activities of the real estate/construction sector include purchase, sale, development of land and residential and non-residential buildings. The real estate/construction sector consists of multiple sub-sectors viz. commercial, residential, hospitality and retail. The residential real estate/construction sector is treated as housing sector. It is important to note that the real estate has come under the purview of the Consumer Protection Act (1986) following an amendment to the definition of 'service' in Section 2(1) (0) of the Act to include the term 'housing construction'. A recent study on the 'impact of investment in housing sector on GDP and Employment in the Indian Economy' (NCAER, 2014: viii), among other things, suggests:
   (1) The residential construction (housing sector) accounts for
      (i) 1.24 per cent of the total output of the economy (total construction sector 11.39%),
      (ii) 1.00 per cent of GDP (total construction sector accounts for 8.2%),

(iii) 6.86 per cent of employment (total construction sector accounts for 11. 52%).

(2) Housing sector is fourth largest employment-generating sector.

(3) 99.41 per cent of jobs in housing sector are informal jobs.

(4) For every lakh invested in the housing sector, 2.69 new jobs (2.65 informal and 0.4 formal) are created. With 'induced effect', the number of jobs created would be 4.06 (3.95 informal and 0.11 formal).

(5) For every investment in housing sector, the household income increases by ₹ 0.41. With 'induced effect', this is estimated to be ₹ 0.76.

(6) Every additional rupee invested in the housing sector will add ₹ 1.54 to the GDP and with household expenditure considered, this is going to add ₹ 2, 84.

(7) For every rupee invested in creation of housing, ₹ 0.12 gets collected as indirect tax.

(8) Labour to output ratio, i.e. the number of persons employed to produce a lakh of units of output, is 2.34 and is the highest among all sectors.

It may be mentioned that the expression 'induced effect' denotes: 'in response to the direct and indirect effects, the level of household income increases due to increased employment and a proportion of this increased income are respent on consumption of final goods and services'.

2. Janaki Nair (2000): A collection of photographs from the project, 'Worlding the City: The Futures of Bangalore' ('Tanks and Tank Beds'), *Beladidc Nodu Bengaluru Nagara*, Centre for the Study of Culture and Society, www.cscsarchive.org: 8081/Bangalore/ Home.nsf

3. As of May 2013, India has 570 operational Malls with a total area of 180 million sq ft compared to just 225 Malls just five years ago. The seven metros (including Bengaluru and Hyderabad) have 190 operational malls. It is not alone that the number of malls has more than doubled since 2008. Also, the average area of the top 15 Malls across the country has gone up 40 per cent (from 6.17 Lakh sq ft to 8.66 Lakh sq ft) in the last three years. Over the next three years, it is projected, the average area of the top 15 Malls would go above 10.3 lakh sq ft. pointing to preference for building larger shopping complexes ('Malls more than double in five years', *Times of India*, Kolkata Edition, 7 August 2013).

4. It is often argued that the development process in India 'appears to have skipped the second stage of economic transition (industrial sector growth), moving directly to growth in the service sector'

(Report, 2012: 1). It is so argued as the contribution of manufacturing sector to India's GDP has remained stagnant at 15–16 per cent. And the resultant manufacturing 'has not contributed perceptibly to tackling the problem of unemployment and under-employment in the unorganized sector'. Steady growth of labour-intensive manufacturing sector could not only add to exports but also initiate changes in employment scenario. While gems and jewellery sector employs about 3.4 million workers (skilled and semi-skilled), it is likely to absorb about 6.6 million workers in various activities by 2018. The leather sector is also a potential sector. This sector has been known for consistency in high export earnings and has created about 2.5 million jobs (direct and indirect) and predominantly for women and weaker sections. The shop-floor operators and workers constitute about 80 per cent of workforce of the industry. An achievement of the exports target of 14 billion US $ by 2016–17 would require an additional workforce of 1 million and of which about 0.8 million would be at the shop-floor level (Report, 2012: 107 and 114).

Realizing the crucial role of manufacturing in earning foreign exchange as well as generation of employment (even in allied sectors), India took a policy decision to raise the share of manufacturing from the current level of 15–16 per cent to 25 per cent of GDP by 2022 and creation of 100 million jobs and the resultant National Manufacturing Policy. The major features of the National Manufacturing Policy (2011) may be mentioned.

The NMP envisages establishment of National Investment and Manufacturing Zones (NIMZs) which will be developed in the nature of green field industrial townships, benchmarked with the best manufacturing hubs in the world. The thrust will be on: employment-intensive industries like gems and jewellery, leather and foot wear and textiles and garments; capital goods industries; industries with strategic significance; industries with competitive advantage; small and medium industries and public sector enterprises. Emphasis will be laid on skill development programmes. There will be an exit policy to remove rigidity in the labour market and to ensure protection of rights of the workers. Efforts will be made to simplify environment laws and regulations. The policy envisages relief from capital gains tax (NMP, 2011: 4–6). Also, the National Manufacturing Policy (NMP), among other things, provides: 1. Relief from Capital Gains Tax on sale of plant and machinery of a unit located in a National Investment and Manufacturing Zone (NIMZ) in case of reinvestment of sale consideration within a period of three years for purchase of new plant and machinery in any other unit located in the same NIMZ or another NIMZ; 2. Rollover relief from long term capital gains tax to individuals on sale of a residential property (house or plot of land) in case of reinvestment of sale consideration in the equity of a new start-up SME company in the manufacturing sector for the purchase of a new plant and machinery; 3. Simple and expeditious exit mechanism for closure of sick units while protecting interest of labour; 4. In respect of environmental laws/regulations, inspection by specially trained/designated/notified agencies for third party inspection to supplement the inspection by the government agencies for compliance monitoring; (PIB: 2014). In order to boost manufacturing sector, it may be mentioned, 16 National Investment and Manufacturing Zones (NIMZs) have already been established (2013–14).

Why has growth of manufacturing been sluggish? Aggarwal has examined this issue at length and has argued: while there were structural constraints that stemmed the growth of manufacturing sector, the structural changes sought or likely to be sought with respect to manufacturing are unlikely to yield desired result. Transformative interventions have been languishing due to indecision, delays and policy reversals. A set of prescriptions have been made for a reversal of the situation. It is argued that adequate attention towards an improvement in manufacturing becomes necessary as manufacturing is central not only to a nation's economy but also the democratic aspirations of her people (Aggarwal, 2014).

5. The Right to Fair Compensation and Transparency in Land Acquisition, Rehabilitation and Resettlement Act, 2013, was enacted to replace the archaic Act of 1894 which suffered from various weaknesses. The Act of 1894 was silent on the issue of resettlement and rehabilitation of those affected by the acquisition of land. The Act of 2013 is an improvement upon the 119 year old Act of 1894 in many respects. The salient features of the Right to Fair Compensation and Transparency in Land Acquisition, Rehabilitation and Resettlement Act, 2013, may be mentioned. These are:

   First, the Right to Fair Compensation and Transparency in Land Acquisition, Rehabilitation and Resettlement Act, 2013 (hereafter the Act), is a comprehensive Act dealing with land acquisition, compensation, rehabilitation and resettlement;

   Second, while land acquisition will require prior consent of 80 per cent of the affected population in case of land to be acquired for private companies, it will require consent of 70 per cent of affected population in case of land to be acquired a project under public private partnership;

   Third, the process of obtaining consent shall be carried out along with Social Impact Assessment study to assess possible impact of the project on multiple components such as livelihood of affected families, assets and infrastructure, public utilities;

   Fourth, the appropriate government, whenever it intends to acquire land for public purpose, it shall consult the concerned Panchayat,

Municipality or Municipal Corporation, as the case may be and will ensure that adequate representation has been given to the institutions of local-self government;

Fifth, the Act includes provisions to safeguard food security;

Sixth, the Act ensures return of the land acquired under the Act, if remains unutilized for a period of five years from the date of taking over the possession, to the original owner, owners or, their legal heirs or to the Land Bank of the appropriate government;

As well, the Act provides guidelines for compensation (Sec26–28) to 'affected families' together with provision for rehabilitation and resettlement (Sec 31, 32, 41, 42 and Schedule II). The Act also envisages that infrastructural facilities will be provided in the Resettlement Area (Gazette of India, 2013).

It needs to be mentioned that the aforesaid Act has not been well taken by a good number of states. A review of the Right to Fair Compensation and Transparency in Land Acquisition, Rehabilitation and Resettlement Act, 2013, has been demanded as the said Act is feared to be a potential impediment to acquisition of land for industrialization. Meanwhile, Medha Patekar, the social activist and the Convener of the National Alliance of People's Movement, argued:

> the consent and Social Impact Assessment provision was introduced to do away with anomalies in the colonial Act since farmers and those dependant on the land were never consulted or made participant in the process of development planning. These new provisions came into being in the wake of protests at places like Nandigram, Singur, Kalinganagar and other places to repeal of the colonial Act (DNA, 2014).

The Right to Fair Compensation and Transparency in Land Acquisition, Rehabilitation and Resettlement (Amendment) Bill, 2015, was adopted by the Lower House (Lok Sabha) with nine amendments. It was not placed in the Upper House (Rajya Sabha). As reported in the Press, the Cabinet has taken a decision to repromulgate the Ordinance. It will be a new one on the Bill that includes the nine amendments. The amended Bill will go back to the Lok Sabha for replacing the (new Ordinance) and then to the Rajya Sabha,' (*The Hindu*, 2015).

Some of the major features of the 'The Right to Fair Compensation and Transparency in Land Acquisition, Rehabilitation and Resettlement (Amendment) Bill, 2015' may be mentioned:

(1) The Bill creates five special categories of land use: 1. defence, 2. rural infrastructure, 3. affordable housing, 4. industrial corridors, and 5. infrastructure projects including Public Private Partnership (PPP) projects where the central government owns the land.

(2) The Bill exempts the five categories from provisions of the LARR Act, 2013, which requires the consent of 80 per cent of land owners to be obtained for private projects and that of 70 per cent of land owners for PPP projects.

(3) The Bill allows exemption for projects in these five categories from requiring Social Impact Assessment imposed by LARR Act 2013.

(4) The Bill brings provisions for compensation, rehabilitation, and resettlement under other related Acts such as the National Highways Act and the Railways Act in consonance with the LARR Act, 2013 (*The Hindu*, 2015a).

6. As quoted in Levien, 2011: 456.
7. It will not be out of place to mention that the generalization of gentrification, as Smith (2002: 441) suggests, has various dimensions which may be understood with reference to five inter-related features. These are: the transformed role of the state, penetration of global finance, changing level of political opposition, geographical dispersal and the sectoral generalization of gentrification. The distinctive feature of the latest phase (third wave) of gentrification in many cities is that 'a new amalgam of corporate and state powers and practices has been forged in a much more ambitious effort to gentrify the city than earlier ones'. Smith adds, 'Most crucially, real-estate development becomes a centerpiece of the city's *productive* economy .... In ways that could hardly have been envisaged in the 1960s, the construction of new gentrification complexes in central cities across the world has become an increasingly unassailable capital accumulation strategy for competing urban economies' (Smith, 2002: 443).

References

Aggarwal, Aradhna (2004): 'Export Processing Zones in India: Analysis of the Export Performance', Working Paper No. 148, Indian Council for Research on International Economic relations, New Delhi.

Aggarwal, Aradhna (2007): 'Impact of Special Economic Zones on Employment, Poverty and Human Development', Working Paper No 194, Indian Council for Research on International Economic relations, New Delhi.

Aggarwal, Aradhna (2014): 'Structural Change and Manufacturing: Changing the Paradigm' in *Stagnant Manufacturing and Policy Slack*. published by IRIS Knowledge Foundation, Mumbai, India jointly with Forum for Global Knowledge Sharing.
http://www.esocialsciences.org/eSS_essay/Manufacturing/Economic%20Growth%20 Structural%20Change.pdf

Aggarwal, O.P. (2006): *India Infrastructure Report, Urban Transport*, Oxford University Press, New Delhi, pp. 106–129.

Amirahamadi, H. and Wu, W (1995): 'Export Processing Zones in Asia', *Asian Survey*, Vol. 35, pp. 828–49.

Baviskar, Amita (2003): 'Between Violence and Desire: Space, Power, and Identity in the Making of Metropolitan Delhi', *International Social Science Journal*, 55, p. 93.

Boyenge, Jean-Pierre Singa (2007): 'ILO Database on Export Processing Zones', Working Paper (251), International Labour Organization, Geneva.

Bhattacharya, Rajesh and Sanyal, Kalyan (2011): 'Bypassing the Squalor: New Towns, Immaterial Labour and Exclusion in Post-colonial Urbanization', *Economic and Political Weekly*, V. XLVI, No. 31, 30 July.

Business-Standard (2014): 'Centre Relaxes Norms for FDI in construction', 30 October.

Carter, L.J. (1985): Walworth 1929–1939, L.J. Carter Services, Surrey (see Preface) as quoted in 'Narrating the City: Spaces of Urban Change, South London' Hall, Suzanne M, LSE Research On Line, p. 11. http://eprints.lse.ac.uk/41643/1/Narrating_the_City%28LSE_RO%29.pdf

Centre for Science and Environment (2011): Citizen's Report: Air Quality and Mobility in Kolkata, Centre for Science and Environment, New Delhi.

Chadah, Sunainaa (2014): 'Easier FDI in Real Estate means Government is Inflating Urban Housing Bubble'. http://www.firstpost.com/business/economy/easier-fdi-in-real-estate-means-govt-is-inflating-indias-urban-housing-bubble-2012111.html

Chatterjee, Piu (2014): 'Urban Villages in Globalized India: Degenerative Growth Processes in Navi Mumbai', *Inclusive* (A Journal of the Kolkata Centre for Contemporary Studies), July 7.

Dittrich, Christopher (2007): 'Bangalore: Globalization and Fragmentation in India's Hightech-Capital', ASIEN 103 (April), pp. 45–58.

DNA (2014): 'Social activist Medha Patkar threatens nationwide stir, opposes change in Land Act', 26 August. http://www.dnaindia.com/india/report-social-activist-medha-patkar-threatens-nationwide-stir-opposes-change-in-land-act-2013967.

Farole, Thomas and Akinci, Gokhan (2011): 'Special Economic Zones, Progress, Emerging Challenges and Future Directions', IBRD/World Bank, Washington DC.

Fernandes, Leela (2004): 'The Politics of Forgetting: Class Politics, State Power and the Restructuring of Urban Space in India', *Urban Studies*, Vol. 41, No. 12, pp. 2415–30.

FIAS (2008): 'Special Economic Zones: Performance, Lessons Learned and Implications for Zone Development', World Bank Group (IBRD), Washington DC.

Gazette of India (2013): 'The Right to Fair Compensation and Transparency in Land Acquisition, Rehabilitation and Resettlement Act 2013', The Gazette of India, Extraordinary, Part II, Section I, No. 40, 27 September, Ministry of Law and Justice (Legislative Branch), GOI.

Glover, William J (2012): 'Construing Urban Space as "Public" in Colonial India: Some Notes from the Punjab'.
http://www.global.ucsb.edu /punjab/journal_14_2/glover.pdf

Harris, A (2008): 'From London to Mumbai and back again: Gentrification and Public Policy in Comparative Perspective' (eprints.uci.ac.uk/14811/1/14811.pdf).

Harvey, David (2006): 'Comment on Commentaries', *Historical Materialism*, 14(4), pp. 157–66 (as quoted in Levien (2011), p. 456).

Harvey, David (2008): 'The Right to the City', *New Left Review*, 53, September–October, pp. 23–40.

The Hindu (2014): 'New Clear Signal to Revive Economic Zones', *Business Line*, 9 July.

The Hindu (2015): 'Land Bill Passed in Lok Sabha', *The Hindu*, 10 March 2015.

The Hindu (2015a): 'Land Bill: Six Important Facts You Need to Know', *The Hindu*, 11 March 2015.

Jamie, Peck, Theodore, Nik and Neil Brenner (2009): SAIS Review vol. XXIX No. 1 (Winter-Spring), pp. 49–66.
http://www.sociology.as.nyu.edu/docs/IO/222/Peck.Theodore.Brenner.2009.pdf

Kappan, Rasheed (2015): 'Those Dangerous Crossings', *Deccan Herald*, 7 May.

Kumar, Ashok (2014): 'A Framework for Gentrification of Indian Cities', *Institute of Town Planners India Journal* 11x1, January–March, pp. 19–32.

Kundu, Amitabh (2007): 'Migration and Urbanization in India in the Context of Poverty Alleviation'.
www.networkideas.org/ideasact/jun07/Beijing.../Amitabh_Kundu.pdf

Kundu, Amitabh (2011): The State of World Population, UNFPA (see, Planning Ahead for the Growth of Cities, Chapter 6, p. 78).
http://foweb.unfpa.org/SWP2011/reports/EN-SWOP2011-FINAL.pdf

Kurien, C.T. (2010): 'On How the Elite Take Over Land in the New Global City' (Review of book) *Accumulation by Dispossession: Transformative Cities in the New Global Order*, edited by Swapna Banerjee-Guha, Sage Publications), *Frontline*, Vol. 27, Issue, 26, 18–31 December.

Lakshmanan, L. (2009): 'Evolution of Special Economic Zones and some Issues: The Indian Experience', Department of Economic Analysis and Policy, Reserve Bank of India, June.
https://www.rbi.org.in/scripts/PublicationReportDetails.aspx?ID=558

Lefebvre, Henri (1970): *The Urban Revolution*, translated by Robert Bononno (2003), University of Minnesota Press, London.

Levien, Michael (2011): 'Special Economic Zones and Accumulation by Dispossession in India', *Journal of Agrarian Change*, Vol. 11, No. 4, October, pp. 454–83.

Manufacturing (2014): Guidelines and Dispensations for Clusters ... under National Manufacturing Policy, Ministry of Commerce and Industry, Government of India.
http://dipp.nic.in/English/policies/guidelines_NIMZ_17January2014.pdf

Menon, S. Narayan and Mitra, Soumya Kanti (2009): 'Special Economic Zones: The Rationale', Occasional Paper (No. 16) in Special Economic Zones: Promise, Performance and Pending Issues, Occasional Paper Series, Centre for Policy Research, New Delhi.

Mirô, Sônia Vives (2011): 'Producing a "Successful City": Neoliberal Urbanism and Gentrification in the Tourist City – The Case of Palma (Majorca)'.
http://www.hindawi.com/journals/usr/2011/989676/

Mohan, Rakesh and Dasgupta, Shubhagato (2005): 'The 21st Century: Asia Becomes Urban', *Economic and Political Weekly*, Vol. 40, No. 3, January 15, pp. 213–223.

Mukherjee, Madhuja (2011): 'Narratives of Development in South Asia: Kolkata, South City and Solace'.
www.kaurab.com/themudproposal/madhuja/narratives.pdf

Nair, Janaki (2006): 'Social Municipalism' and the New Metropolis', in *Contested Transformations: Changing Economies and Identities in India*, edited by Mary E. John, Praveen Kumar Jha and Surinder S. Jodhka; Tulika Books, New Delhi.

Nair, Janaki (2005): *The Promise of the Metropolis: Bangalore's Twentieth Century*, Oxford University Press (Paperback Edition), New Delhi.

NCAER (2014): Impact of Investments in the Housing Sector on GDP and Employment in the Indian Economy, National Council of Applied Economic Research, New Delhi.
http://mhupa.gov.in/W_new/Impact_of_Housing_on_GDP_Employment_FULL_REPORT.pdf

Narayan, M. (2010): 'ICT Sector, Globalization and Urban Economic Growth: Evidences from Bangalore', Working Paper (2010/80), July, UNU-WIDER.

NMP (2011): National Manufacturing Policy, Government of India. http://dipp.nic.in/English/policies/National_Manufacturing_Policy_25October2011.pdf

PIB (2014): 'National Investment and Manufacturing Zones', Press Information Bureau, GOI. http://pib.nic.in/newsite/PrintRelease.aspx? relid=103390

Ramkrishnan, Kavita (2013): 'City Futures: Aspirations and Urban Imaginaries in Delhi', *Kaleidoscope 5*. 1 January, pp. 100–108 (Institute of Advanced Study, Durham University).

Rawat, Vidya Bhushan et al. (2011): 'The Impact of Special Economic Zones in India: A Case Study of Ponepally SEZ' (Paper presented at the International Conference on Global Land Grabbing, University of Sussex, 6–8 April), Social Development Foundation, New Delhi.

Report (2012): Report of the Working Group on Boosting India's Manufacturing Exports, Twelfth Five Year Plan (2012–17), Department of Commerce, Ministry of Commerce, GOI.

Samaddar, Ranabir (2011): 'Rajarhat, the Urban Dystopia', 29 July 2011. http://mail.sarai.net/pipermail/reader-list_mail.sarai.net/2011August/028740.html, (see also, Samaddar, Ranabir, Ishita Dey, Suhit K Sen (2013) *Beyond Kolkata: Rajarhat and the Dystopia of Urban Imagination*, Routledge India).

Smith, Neil (2002): 'New Globalism, New Urbanism: Gentrification as Global Urban Strategy', *Autopode*, Blackwell Publisher, UK, pp. 427–450.

Smith, Neil (2003): (Foreword) *The Urban Revolution*, Lefebvre, Henri (2003), translated by Robert Bononno, University of Minnesota Press, London (p. VII-XXIII).

Swyngedouw, Erik, Frank Moulaert and Arantxa Rodriguez (2002): 'Neoliberal Urbanization in Europe', *Antipode*, Vol. 34 (3), pp 543–577, Blackwell, USA (as quoted in Banerjee-Guha, Swapna (2009): 'Neoliberalising the 'Urban': New Geographies of Power and Injustice in Indian Cities', *Economic and Political Weekly*, Vol. 44 (22), pp. 95–107.

Tantri, Malini L. (2010): 'Effectiveness of SEZs over EPZs Structure: The Performance at Aggregate Level', Working Paper 248, The Institute for Social and Economic Change, Bangalore.

Times of India (2014): 'UPA's Land Acquisition Law Likely to be Overhauled with Many State Seeking Recast', 28 June. http://timesofindia.indiatimes.com/india/UPAs-land-acquisition-law-likely-to-be-overhauled-with-many-states-seeking-recast/articleshow/

Times of India (2013): 'Malls more than double in five years', Kolkata Edition, August 7.

CHAPTER 2

State and Urban Housing

Policies, Priorities and Progress

Despite some 'degree of earnestness' on the part of the state in independent India in transforming the state of urban housing, the end result, or the outcome, of state intervention does not allow to become contented. This is not to argue that nothing has been done. Rather, more has to be done and at greater pace given the fact that urbanization in India has been taking place faster than anticipated.

Introduction

Urbanization inevitably accompanies promises as well as challenges. Usual it is, urbanization leads to growth in demand for housing of all varieties (low-cost to high-end) surpassing the supply. Transformative intervention to offset the urbanization-driven crisis of housing becomes necessary. The cities across societies witness transformative intervention in addressing the urbanization-induced challenges. The sewerage and waste disposal system was introduced in the city of London to contain deteriorating public health due to enormous growth of London-based industries and metropolitan population during the late nineteenth century. In British India, initiative had been taken to improve the sanitary situation in three Presidencies viz.; Madras, Bombay and Calcutta. The twenty-first century urban India witnessed the launching of Jawaharlal Nehru National Urban Renewal Mission (JNNURM) aimed at 'fast-track planned development of identified cities'.

Desire for housing transcends time, class and culture. It is chiefly because housing, an 'asset with embedded value that keeps appreciating', promises 'enhanced financial stability and social inclusion'. The major concern of the present chapter has been to critically address the policies and priorities of the state in regard to urban housing in independent India and the end result of such initiatives. The particular focus has been housing for those who are at the lower end of income distribution. The present chapter consists of five small segments. The initiatives of the state in independent India towards urban housing have been described in Section II and Section III. While Section II reflects on the situation during the period between India's independence and adoption of the New Economic Policy, Section III examines the post-reform situation with particular focus on the National Housing Policies. Section IV dwells on the priorities of the state as revealed through the National Housing Policies (1988, 1994, 1998 and 2007). Section V concerns the end result or, the outcome of state intervention with respect to urban housing in post-colonial India. The discussion that follows begins with a brief reference to the state of urban poor in colonial India (Section I).

Urban Poor in Colonial India

In colonial India, overcrowding and insanitation were the common features of the major cities like Calcutta, Karachi, Ahmedabad, Cawnpore and also Mumbai where, in the wake of plague, the first Improvement Trust was established at the close of the nineteenth century (1890). In 1890, apart from living in abysmal condition, there were around 1,00,000 homeless labourers who 'sleep at night in open spaces on footpaths or on verandahs of houses, in temple compounds and in masjids, dharamshalas, etc.' (Kidambi, 2007). The Bombay Improvement Trust was a failed initiative,

> In pursuing its goal of improving slums – or destroying them – and making available better living conditions for the poor. At least, in the short run, the trust was actually reducing the supply of low cost accommodation, and doing it, without concern for those evicted. Thousands of houses were destroyed without alternative being provided (Spodek, 2013: 58).

There is no reason to believe that the situation in Calcutta, the 'second city' of the British Empire, was better. Calcutta had the highest percentage of slums of any city in India.[1] 'The physical condition of the native sections of Calcutta were apparently even worse than Bombay's and the city suffered from high rates of illness, disease and death ... Calcutta had the highest percentage of slums of any city in India' (Spodek, 2013: 58).

The most notable spatial divide in colonial Calcutta was between 'the colonizers (living in high amenity, well serviced areas) and the natives (living in unplanned, congested and poorly serviced areas)' (Chakravorty, 2000: 65). The state of living in colonial India during late nineteenth century in the northern parts of Calcutta, the native parts of the town, is reflected in the account of C. Fabre-Tonnerre, the Health Officer for the Calcutta Municipality (1872)[2]:

> A *bustee* or native village generally consists of a mass of huts constructed without any plan or arrangement, without roads, without drains, ill-ventilated and never cleaned. Most of these villages are the abodes of misery, vice, and filth, and the nurseries of sickness and disease. In these *bustees* are found green and slimy stagnant ponds, full of putrid vegetable and animal matter in a state of decomposition and whose bubbling surfaces exhale, under a tropical sun, noxious gases, poisoning the atmosphere and spreading around disease and death. These ponds supply the natives with water for domestic purposes and are very often the receptacles of filth .... The huts are huddled together in masses and pushed to the very edge of the ponds, their projecting eaves often meeting together, whilst the intervening spaces, impervious to the rays of the sun, are converted into necessaries and used by both sexes in common. In these huts often live entire families, the members of which occupy the single apartment of which it is not infrequently composed, and in which they cook, eat, and sleep together; the wet and spongy floor, with a mat spread on it serving as a bed for the whole.

It was a well-known fact, Tonnerre added, 'that many of the epidemics that visited Calcutta ... first made their appearance in the northern division of the town'.[3]

That the 'need for action for an improvement in the situation was immediate' had been advocated by many scholars and town planners. While physical planning was suggested as an effective remedy, so was social planning and engineering. Radhakamal Mukherjee, the proponent of the social planning and engineering model, had the apprehension that the enormous surplus of male population in industrial cities might otherwise be attracted to 'liquor shops and brothels where there is more room space, more light and more company' (Bogle, 1929). The situation after the World War II deteriorated further, 'overcrowded, squalid conditions of living became sharply pronounced' (Ranganathan, 2011: 166).

Measures like supply of filtered water to the inhabitants and introduction of underground drainage system had been initiated to improve the situation in colonial Kolkata. 'Of course, the progress of areas covered by water and sewerage treatment meant that Europeans gained benefits first, followed by middle-class Indians, and finally the poor' (Beattie, 2013: 13).

One reason for relative indifference to welfare of the urban poor could be that the colonial ruler bothered least about securing support of the urban poor as collaborator to the British administration. The urban poor were labelled as 'corrupted misfits' to the urban environment and a threat to order and stability and by implication, progress. The colonial perception of the urban poor used to influence the policy measures vis-à-vis the urban poor 'which remained largely oriented towards discipline, regulation and segregation and often in alliance with the Indian elite'. And, 'these tendencies were most clearly reflected in local policies and policing which encompassed attempts to control the behaviour of the poor, clear their slum settlements and regulate their collective activities' (Gooptu, 2001: 13).

Debate continues, whether or not, the public health measures, undertaken in colonial India, were effectively used as a 'tool for the domination of indigenous people and demonstration of colonial benevolence intended to reduce resistance to imperial rule' (Harrisson, 1994: 3). Presumably, strong apprehension of infection from the indigenous population would allow strengthening the rationale for segregated residential pattern in colonial India (Harrisson, 1994: 3).

Post-Independence India

Five-Year Plans

The unprecedented partition-induced influx of refugees from both West Pakistan and East Pakistan (now Bangladesh) led to sudden and substantial addition to the then (particularly urban) population of India. The urban population increased by 53.7 per cent between

1941 and 1951. Apart from unprecedented partition-induced influx of refugees, the substantial increase in the urban population was a result of the war-induced opportunities for employment in cities during the World War II (Batra, 2009: 5). The cities experienced proliferation of 'sub-standard' housing and slums. The First Five Year Plan recorded:

> Most of the towns in India ... have a large proportion of sub-standard houses and slums containing insanitary mud-huts of flimsy construction, poorly ventilated, over-congested and often lacking in essential amenities such as water and light. This is specially so in the large industrial cities (Dwivedi, 2007: 34).

According to one estimate, the shortage in urban housing stood at 18.4 lakh excluding 10 lakh housing units estimated to be required for refugees from Pakistan (Dwivedi, 2007: 41). It will not be out of place to mention that the states like Tripura, Bihar or Assam were also afflicted by the problem of partition-induced refugees apart from Punjab and Bengal. However, forced migration in Punjab and Bengal has been known for their own region-specific distinctions. As Bose argues:

> The intensity and depth of violence in the West was much more than the East but here mayhem and displacement remained confined to first three years. In Bengal, on the contrary, refugee flow remains a continuous affair and has become an inescapable part of its reality (Bose, 2010: 8).

Accommodating the surplus and dispossessed population was indeed a great challenge to India, the just-born nation. The housing sector, among 'many competing demands on limited resources', was accorded priority. The sector received more than one-third of the total allocation of the First Five Year Plan (1951–56). A sizeable part of the plan outlay had been spent on rehabilitation of the refugees from Pakistan and building the new city of Chandigarh. An Industrial Housing Scheme was launched.

That urbanization could be widespread and that the cities could be an engine of economic growth, as it has already been indicated, were not adequately appreciated by the then policy makers and planners in India. Hence, the urbanization-induced challenges like housing 'were treated more as welfare problems and sectors of residual investment rather than as issues of national economic importance'.

A review of the policies and programmes for housing pursued in successive Five Year Plans suggest that emphasis was laid on improvement in housing condition for the economically disadvantaged groups in all subsequent plans. Between 1952 and 2011, the urban India witnessed launching of a host of housing schemes for the vulnerable segments in the society (the Economically Weaker Section (EWS) and the Low Income Groups (LIG))[4] beginning with the Integrated Subsidized Housing Scheme for Industrial Workers and the EWS in 1952 to Rajiv Awas Yojana (RAY) in 2011 (Table 22). During the Second Five Year Plan (1956–61), the scope of housing programme for the poor was expanded and the Industrial Housing Scheme was widened to cover all workers. A Scheme was introduced in 1959 to extend loans to the state governments. for a period of 10 years for acquisition and development of land to ensure that sufficient number of building sites are available. The Third Five Year Plan (1961–66) put emphasis on co-ordination of efforts of all agencies and orienting the programmes to the needs of the LIGs. Master Plans for major cities had been prepared. The Fourth Five Year Plan (1969–74) stressed the need for creation of smaller towns and spatial location of economic activities to prevent further growth of population in large cities. Decongestion or dispersal of population was felt necessary (Ministry, 2007). The Fifth Five Year Plan (1974–79) put thrust on developing small and medium towns hoping that development of medium and small towns might help in reducing the growing pressure of urbanization on large cities. Controlling urban land price, extending provision for basic amenities in cities and towns were also accorded priority. The Urban Land (Ceiling and Regulation) Act, 1976, was enacted to contain increasing urban land price. It was thought that the said Act, apart from containing upward trend in price of urban land, would ensure 'equitable distribution of land among various social classes and an orderly development of built-environment' (Batra, 2009: 13). The end result or, outcome of the said Act was, however, disappointing (UH-HABITAT, 2008: 7). The Urban Land (Ceiling and Regulation) Act, 1976, did not 'ensure redistribution of land but it created opportunities for speculative buying of urban land and thereby making the prices shot up further. The distribution of land became even more skewed to the advantage of the urban elite' (Batra, 2009: 15).

Table 22

Urban Housing Schemes of GOI (1952–2011)

S. No.	Scheme	Year of Launch
1.	Integrated Subsidized Housing Scheme for Industrial Workers and EWS	1952
2.	LIG Housing Scheme	1954
3.	MIG Housing Scheme	1959
4.	Rental Housing Scheme for state government employees	1959
5.	Slum Clearance and Improvement Scheme	1959
6.	Environmental improvement of urban slums	1972
7.	Night Shelter Scheme for pavement dwellers	1990
8.	National Slum Development Programme (NSDP)	1996
9.	Two Million Housing Scheme	1998
10.	Valmiki Ambedkar Awas Yojana (VAMBAY)	2001
11.	Jawaharlal Nehru National Urban Renewal Mission* (JNNURM)	2005
12.	Basic Services to Urban Poor (BSUP)	2005
13.	Integrated Housing and Slum Development Programme** (IHSDP)	2005
14.	Affordable Housing in Partnership (AHIP)	2007
15.	Interest Subsidy Scheme for Housing the Urban Poor (ISHUP)	2009
16.	Rajiv Awas Yojana*** (RAY)	2011

* JNNURM was launched in 2005 with the aim to build 1.5 million houses for urban poor during the mission period, 2005–12. It had a couple of sub-missions viz.; BSUP (to provide seven basic services/entitlements (security of tenure, affordable housing, water, sanitation, health, education and social security) to LIG in 65 mission cities) and IHSDP (to provide above basic services/entitlements to LIG in towns and cities other than the 65 mission cities).

** The schemes viz.; VAMBAY and NSDP were subsumed in the IHSDP after it was launched in 2005.

*** In pursuance of the vision of 'Slum-Free India', RAY was launched in 2011. It was planned that RAY would be made effective in two phases: Preparatory (that ended in 2013) and Implementation. The GOI has approved the implementation phase for the period 2013–22. The existing schemes viz.; AHIP and ISHUP have been dovetailed into RAY.

Source: 'Transformation of Housing Policies in India-Trend Towards Market Mechanisms' (Rao, 2004: 4) (http://118.143.90.144/hdw/ihc/pdf/rhk.pdf); Guidelines for various Urban Housing Schemes sponsored by the Government of India.

The Sixth Plan (1980–85) facilitated launching of the centrally-sponsored scheme called Integrated Development of Small and Medium Towns (IDSMT) with the objective of promoting growth in towns with less than 0.1 million population by way of providing basic services and infrastructural development. It was thought that the strategy of massive relocation of slums in urban areas 'not only involves substantial hardship to those affected in terms of loss of easy access to employment centre and other amenities, but results in unnecessary destruction of existing housing capital, however sub-standard it may be' (6th Plan 1980). With the change in government at the centre, the Sixth Plan (1978–83) was terminated in 1980 only to be replaced by the new Sixth Plan (1980–85).

The Seventh Five Year Plan (1985–90) was a departure in the sense that it argued for shifting the major responsibility of housing construction to the private sector. The Seventh Plan emphasized:

> The major responsibility of housing construction would have to be left to the private sector, in particular the household sector .... The time has now come for the government to set before itself a clear goal in the field of housing ... not so much to build but to promote housing activity (Seventh Plan, 1985).

To augment the flow of institutional finance to the housing sector and promoting and regulating the housing finance institutions, the National Housing Bank (NHB) was set up in 1988 under the National Housing Bank Act, 1987. The setting up of the National Housing Bank heralded the era of formal housing finance system in India. The state was assigned the role of mobilization of resources for housing, making provision for subsidized housing for the poor and acquisition and development of land (NHB a, 2012). That the primary role of the state would be that of a facilitator and more market-friendly reforms are needed to ensure inflow of private investment to this sector were corroborated by subsequent Five Year Plans. This is with the exception that the state may need to intervene to provide housing to EWS and LIG (UN-HABITAT, 2008: 12)

Co-operative Housing

In India, the co-operative housing movement started at the beginning of the twentieth century. Bangalore Building

Co-operative Society, the first housing co-operative in India, was born in 1909. Later in 1913, the State of Bombay (presently, the state of Maharashtra) took a decision to set up a non-official body, the Bombay Co-operative Housing Association. And, it was the first one to receive financial participation of the state in the affairs of housing co-operatives. This organization had a crucial role in the propagation of co-operative housing. Until the 1950s, the progress of co-operative housing was, however, limited as the legal and the administrative frameworks were inadequately supportive.

A couple of events chiefly contributed to reverse the trend in growth of housing co-operatives in independent India. These were: first, Pt. Nehru envisioned the growth of co-operatives as 'part of his paradigm of democratic socialism' and second, the Working Group on Housing Cooperatives (1964) endorsed the view that housing co-operatives would be the 'best means to provide decent houses at affordable prices' to those at the lower end of income distribution (ICA, 2012: 39). The National Cooperative Housing Federation of India (NCHF), the apex organization of entire co-operative housing movement in the country, was set up (1969) based upon the recommendation of the Working Group on Housing Cooperatives. NCHF, since its inception, has been engaged in promoting, developing and coordinating the activities of the housing cooperatives. As of 2009–10, the number of the primary housing co-operatives has increased to about 0.1 million with a membership of seven million (Table 23, Figure 1). A recent study, undertaken by NCHF, reveals that 11 out of every 100 houses thus far constructed in India and by all types of institutions in the public, private and co-operative sector, have been facilitated by the housing co-operatives (NCHF, 2012: 1).

State Housing Board

The State Housing Boards started emerging in the 1960s. A shift in housing policy greatly hastened the emergence of the State Housing Boards. It was decided during the Second Five Year Plan (1956–61) that direct assistance would be provided to the states for developing housing for low-income groups in lieu of providing loan to the low-income groups. The Third Five Year Plan (1961–66) and the triennial Plan (1966–69) also put thrust on housing for low-income groups in urban areas. In order to meet the challenge of need of housing of the low-income groups, the resources of the State Housing Boards were increased with the expectation that the shortage of housing would be effectively addressed by the State Housing Boards in their respective states (UN-HABITAT 2008: 11). In India, presently, about 17 State Housing Boards are engaged in building houses for various economic groups with financial support from a variety of sources. In commensurate with the pace of urbanization and the resultant growth in demand for housing and civic services, several State Housing Boards introduced changes in structure and strategies. The Maharashtra Housing Board and West Bengal Housing Board may illustrate the situation. Maharashtra Housing Board, formerly called 'Bombay Housing Board', was established in the year 1948 to undertake construction of residential buildings under various housing schemes for different sections of the society. In 1977, Maharashtra Housing and Area Development Authority came into existence through the passage of the Maharashtra Housing and Area Development Act, 1976. It was again re-structured in 1992 and split into three separate Boards viz.; Mumbai Housing and Area Development Board, Mumbai Buildings Repair and Reconstruction Board and Mumbai Slum Improvement Board (MHADA 2014).

Table 23

Trend in Growth of Working Capital, Membership and Primary Societies of Housing Co-operatives in India (1979–80/2009–10)

	Trend in Growth (1979–80/2009–10)					
	1979–80	*1983–84*	*1995–96*	*1999–2000*	*2008–09*	*2009–10*
*Working Capital	12,477	15,000	43,500	92,219	1,25,549.8	1,25,438.1
*Membership	1.9	3	6	6.5	7	7
Primary Societies	34,052	40,000	90,000	92,000	1,00,000	1,00,000

* Working Capital and Membership in Million.

Source: Indian Cooperative Movement: A Statistical Profile (2012: 71), National Cooperative Union of India, New Delhi.

Figure 1

Trend in Growth of Housing Co-operatives and Membership

Year	*1979–80*	*1983–84*	*1995–96*	*1999–2k*	*2008–09*	*2009–10*
Membership	1.9	3	6	6.5	7	7

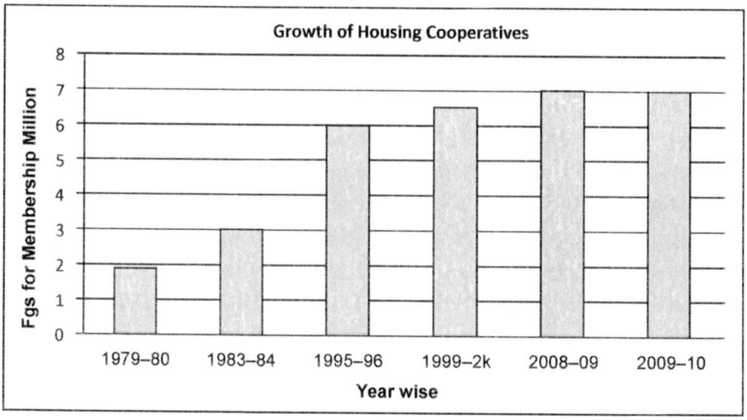

Source: Indian Cooperative Movement: A Statistical Profile, 2012.

The West Bengal State Housing Board decided to undertake joint venture projects with the private builders. It was felt that the initiatives of the State Housing Boards were thus far inadequate in coping with the growing demand for urban housing in particular. The prospective buyers in the housing market had no choice other than approaching the private promoters. Dissatisfaction with price, quality and ownership were growing among the buyers. The joint sector companies in housing sector emerged at this juncture. There are nine joint sector companies and 10 assisted sector companies.[5] These joint sector companies are required to construct 50 per cent of the total number of units constructed for the LIG and MIG category. Majority of the joint sector companies in housing sector emerged in the 1990s and these agreed to build houses for various income groups with the 'provision of cross-subsidization through the premium earned on sale proceeds of HIG and commercial spaces'.

Housing and Urban Development Corporation

The 1970s witnessed a couple of significant developments. First, establishment of Housing and Urban Development Corporation Limited (HUDCO), a fully owned enterprise of the Government of India (under the companies ACT 1956), to 'assist and promote housing and urban development programmes with a special focus on the needs for the economically weaker sections and low income groups' and second, emergence of Housing Development Finance Corporation (HDFC), a pioneer in providing housing loan to 'individuals, groups and cooperative societies as well as companies for staff housing'. HUDCO is mainly engaged in financing housing (both urban and rural) and urban infrastructure. HUDCO has consistently taken initiatives towards social housing. About 94 per cent beneficiaries of total housing units sanctioned by HUDCO belong to the EWS and LIG categories (Annual Report, 2012–13: 79–88). HUDCO has been a critical partner to various GOI-sponsored schemes (housing and basic services) launched for the urban poor and these include: Basic Services for Urban Poor, Integrated Housing and Slum Development Programme, Integrated Subsidy Scheme for Housing for Urban Poor and Rajiv Awas Yojana.

National Housing Policies

The independent India had to wait long four decades for the first National Housing Policy (1988) to be announced. It could be a coincidence but the Global Shelter Strategy was adopted by the UN in the same year. The long term goal of the first National Housing Policy (1988) was:

> To eradicate houselessness, improve the housing conditions of the inadequately housed and provide a minimum level of basic services and amenities to all. The role of Government was conceived, as a provider for the poorest and vulnerable sections and as a facilitator for other income groups and private sector by the removal of constraints and the increased supply of land and services (NHB a, 2012).

Three National Policies on Housing were announced after the onset of the process of economic reforms in India. These were: National Housing Policy (1994), National Housing and Habitat Policy (1998) and National Urban Housing and Habitat Policy

(2007). These National Housing Policies have been instrumental in initiating significant reforms in housing sector. It is best put in some detail.

With the change in government at the centre, a new National Housing Policy was announced in 1994. The National Housing Policy (1994) focused on housing towards comprehensive well-being of rural and urban population. The existing housing schemes, sponsored by the Government of India, for the urban poor were assured of necessary assistance. The National Housing and Habitat Policy (1998), a 'subsequent version' of the National Housing Policy (1994), among others, advocated for changed role of the stakeholders; repeal of the Urban Land Ceiling Act; ensuring Foreign Direct Investment in housing sector; encouragement to private and cooperative sectors for greater participation through fiscal incentives and continued role of the state in provisioning housing for the poor.

At least a couple of major developments in the 1990s, with crucial implications for the urban housing sector, demand particular attention. These are: (i) increasing role of private investment in housing and infrastructure and, (ii) involvement of the Commercial Banks and Housing Finance Institutions. In tune with India's expressed commitment to encourage greater participation of the private sector in the process of economic development, the National Housing Policies and the Five Year Plans announced in post-reform India, have favoured a shift in the role of the state from provider to facilitator with respect to the housing sector (exception being the affordable segment, where state intervention may be necessary). Table 24 indicates growing dominance of the private sector in housing sector.

Since the 1990s, an appreciable progress in institutional housing finance in India was evident. This had become possible chiefly because of involvement of the commercial banks. With aggressive participation of the commercial banks, the housing finance companies have lost their traditional domination in the housing finance market. 'Nearly 80 per cent of the housing stock would be financed from informal sources' prior to setting up of the National Housing Bank (RBI, 2009: 191). There were only a couple of formal housing finance companies (to be specific, HUDCO and

HDFC) before the National Housing Bank was born in 1988. But HUDCO, a state-owned company, as it has already been stated, had been established to finance the state-initiated schemes on housing and infrastructure development. HDFC, a private company, established in 1977, remained engaged in providing housing finance in non-state sector (individuals to corporate housing).

Table 24

Capital Expenditure on Housing under Five Year Plan (in ₹ billion)

Five-Year Plan Period	*Public Investment*	*Private Investment*	*Total Investment*
1st (1951–56)	2.50	9.00	11.50
2nd (1956–61)	3.00	10.00	13.00
3rd (1961–66)	4.25	11.25	15.50
4th (1969–74)	6.25	21.75	28.00
5th (1974–79)	7.96	36.40	44.36
6th (1980–85)	14.91	180.00	194.91
7th (1985–90)	24.58	290.00	314.58
8th (112–97)	315.00	660.00	975.00
9th (1997–02)	520.00	990.00	1,510.00
10th (2003–07)	4,150.00	3,113.00	7,263.00*

* Estimated figure as per plan document.

Source: 'Trend and Progress Report 2003', National Housing Bank. (Cited in 'Housing Finance Mechanism in India' UN-HABITAT, 2008: 12, Nairobi)

With the setting up of the National Housing Bank, many new Housing Finance Companies, including several those sponsored by banks and financial institutions, emerged reinforcing the trend in formal housing finance in India. Large corporate houses and multi-national companies have recently entered into the housing finance business. As of 31 March 2013, the number of registered housing finance companies has increased to 56 (NHB, 2013: 10). Undeniably, these changes have endowed the 'aspiring potential home-owners with access to housing finance and facilitated home ownership in a big way' (RBI, 2009: 192). Rapidly increasing shortage of urban housing and growth of slums at an alarming rate influenced the decision to announce an urban-specific National Housing Policy. Eventually, the National Urban Housing and Habitat Policy (2007) appeared. It was announced at a time when the estimated shortage of urban housing soared to 24.71 million. The EWS and the LIG were found most vulnerable segments (Table 25, Figure 2). The thrust of the National Urban Housing and Habitat Policy (2007) was on ensuring 'Affordable Housing For All' with special emphasis on social housing for the EWS/LIG categories. Shifting in role of the state and involvement of multiple stake-holders were emphasized. The Preamble to the National Urban Housing and Habitat Policy (2007) reads thus:

> Given the magnitude of housing Shortage and budgetary constraints of both the Central and the State Governments, it is amply clear that public sector efforts will not suffice in fulfilling the housing demand. In view of this scenario, the Policy focuses the spotlight on multiple stakeholders ... the Policy will seek to promote various types of public-private partnerships for realizing the goal of Affordable Housing For All (NUHHP, 2007: 1).

Key Priorities

A close look at the National Housing Policies reveals the key priorities of the state vis-à-vis urban housing. The key priorities of the state may be identified as:

Table 25

Distribution of Housing Shortage by Economic Category (2007)

Economic Category	*Distribution of Housing Shortage by Economic Category (2007)*	
	No. (in Millions)	*In Percentage*
EWS	21.78	88.14
LIG	2.89	11.70
MIG and Above	0.04	0.16
Total	24.71	100.00

Figure 2

Housing Shortage in Millions in 2007

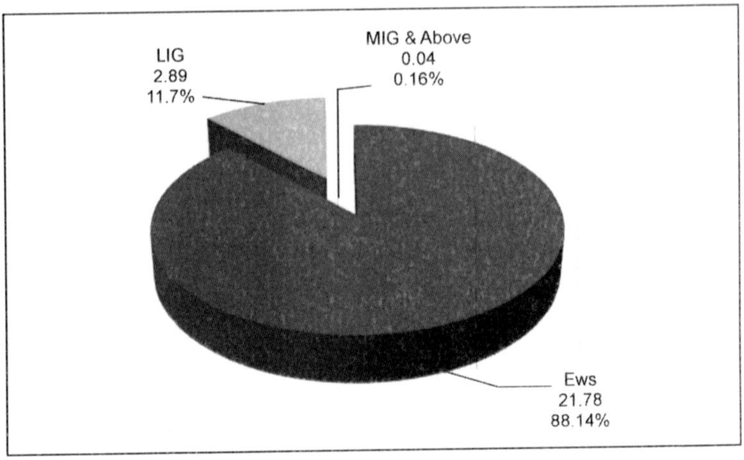

Source: 'Report of the Technical Group (2007–12) on Estimation of Urban Housing Shortage', Ministry of Housing and Urban Poverty Alleviation, GOI.

1. 'Affordable Housing For All' with particular emphasis on vulnerable sections of society.
2. Shift in role of the state from provider to enabler/facilitator (except in case of social housing).
3. Encouragement to Foreign Direct Investment in housing and infrastructure.

Each of these key priorities is described, in some detail, below.

Affordable Housing[6]

Urban India chronically suffers from shortage of housing. Economically weaker and low-income families continue to be the worst sufferers. These groups are hopelessly marginalized in urban housing market. Also, the degraded habitats, in which the urban poor are constrained to live, make them susceptible to frequent illness. In order to cope with these situations, it was envisaged that 'the housing stock is improved through urban renewal, in situ slum improvement and development of new housing stock in existing cities as well as new townships' (NUHHP, 2007: 6). In order to provide basic services to the urban poor, the scheme entitled, Basic Services for the Urban Poor (BSUP), had been launched, as part of

JNNURM, in low-income settlements of 65 mission cities. An identical scheme, launched for the (non) mission cities, was known as the Integrated Housing and Slum Development Programme (IHSDP).

It was realized that the major constraint to making affordable housing available to the urban poor is availability of urban land. Accordingly, a new scheme, entitled 'Affordable Housing in Partnership', was launched in 2009 and as part of JNNURM. It was intended 'to encourage the state governments to make provision for land to meet the acute shortage of affordable housing and to work in the partnership model as envisaged in the National Urban Housing and Habitat Policy' (2007). It was decided that the dwelling units would be a mix of EWS/LIG/MIG categories and that sale price of the dwelling units should have an upper ceiling in terms of rupees per sq. mt. of carpet area. As well, the state would retain its original role of a provider in social housing so that 'affordable housing is made available to the EWS and LIG categories'.

Role-Shift

Going by the Seventh Five Year Plan (1985–90) document, it may be argued, the groundwork for shifting the responsibility of housing construction to the private sector was already prepared. The NUHHP (2007) made it amply clear. The said Policy affirmed intensification of the role of the state as a 'facilitator' and 'regulator' but with 'retaining its role in social housing' to make certain that affordable housing is made available to the EWS/LIG of the population (NUHHP, 2007: 9).

Should state retain its original role of a producer-provider? Or, should it act as an enabler/facilitator? Debate continues over the appropriate role of the state in addressing the issue of housing under changing situations when the state appears to be too keen to substantially reduce its welfare obligations on the one hand and increasing pressure for reform in legislative and regulatory framework and institutional support to the market-needs on the other. While debate over the appropriate role of the state continues, it is undeniable, primacy has to be accorded to substantial reduction in shortage of housing for the EWS/LIG/MIG categories and to make them able to afford and have an access to housing built for them. The state needs to adopt pro-active stance vis-à-vis housing for the urban poor, EWS/LIG/MIG categories and more particularly, given the fact that affordable housing schemes do not appear 'attractive' to the private investors. It is chiefly because the construction costs of affordable housing project are reasonably higher compared to that of luxury projects. According to one estimate, 'construction costs form nearly 50 per cent to 60 per cent of the total selling price in affordable housing projects while for luxury projects this figure is 18 per cent to 20 per cent'. Again, availing a home loan in the range of ₹ 3 lakh to 5 lakh becomes a problem. The housing finance agencies including the banks conceive a home loan between ₹ 3 lakh and ₹ 5 lakh as 'high risk'. The apprehension of the housing finance agencies deprives the poor of availing a home loan to meet their needs (La Salle, 2012). Additionally, as it has been elaborated later, that pre-revised FDI Guidelines for investment in real estate sector (housing and infrastructure) had discouraging effect on the private investors in affordable housing segment.

Foreign Direct Investment

Encouragement to Foreign Direct Investment (FDI) in housing and infrastructure has been the other key priority. India is not a stranger to foreign investment. External finance capital (European) dominated the Indian economy and particularly the primary extractive industry until India won independence (Mukhopadhyay, 2005). Yet, the approach of independent India to foreign capital 'has been varied between political independence and economic liberalization'. The already worsening situation in balance of payments with current account deficit, the Gulf crisis, fall in foreign exchange remittance, increasing oil bill all combined to adversely impact upon India's reserve of foreign exchange to push India on the brink of external debt fault. 'Withdrawal of non-resident deposits to the tune of $952 million' between March and June 1991, led to further drop in India's foreign reserve. As of June 1991, the foreign currency assets of RBI stood to finance three weeks import (Rangarajan, 2001). India decided to bring in reforms in her economy. Needless to say, the adoption of the New Economic Policy in 1991 was in harmony with the growing interest of the global capital about the emerging markets.

Foreign Direct Investment was permitted to the extent of 100 per cent (through automatic route) in township, housing, built-up infrastructure and construction development projects (including housing, commercial premises, hotels, resorts, hospitals, educational institutions) subject to certain conditions in terms of the minimum land area, the built-up area, the capitalization and the lock-in period. The guidelines of FDI in housing and infrastructure (the minimum land area, the built-up area, the capitalization and the lock-in period) existed with discouraging effects for FDI in the affordable housing segment in particular. The Affordable Housing projects, for example, would require a layout size much less than the minimum specified amount of 10 hectares. Again, there was the condition of minimum lock-in period (three years). These and such other riders had discouraging effect for the potential foreign investors. As it has already been stated, necessary policy decision has been announced with regard to relaxation in FDI norms for the construction sector. Such a shift in policy decision has been made obviously with the hope that relaxation of FDI norms in the construction sector would not only boost up this sector of the economy but also would attract more investment in the affordable segment. Discrimination in terms of levying of Service Tax is yet another issue that interferes with inflow of investment in Affordable Housing segment. While investment in Affordable Housing units, built as part of JNNURM and Rajiv Awas Yojana (RAY), are exempted from Service Tax, the Affordable Housing units built by the private developers, NOT as part of either of the above Schemes, do not enjoy any such exemption (Real Estate, 2012: 28–31).

Progress in Housing

The housing policies and subsequent interventions of the state obviously reflect some degree of earnestness on its part in transforming the state of housing for the urban poor in particular. The end result, or the outcome however, does not allow becoming contented despite these transformative initiatives.

It is true that urban housing shortage has plunged from 24.7 million in 2007 (the beginning year of the 11th five year plan) to 18.78 million in 2012 (the beginning year of the Twelfth Five Year Plan). But it is also true that shortage of housing for all economic categories has significantly increased between 2007 and 2012 with the exception of the EWS. Again, more than 95 per cent of urban housing shortage still remains for those who are at the lower end of income distribution, although, indicating an improvement upon the situation in 2007 when it was 99.83 per cent (Table 26, Figure 3). Moreover, the size of urban populace, living in severely congested houses requiring new homes, has increased significantly from 12.67 million to 14.88 million. The size of urban population living in obsolescent house has improved marginally from 02.39 million to 2.27 million (Table 27). As well, while the shortage of housing for the EWS has decreased substantially from 21.78 million in 2007 to 10.55 million in 2012, the shortage of housing for the Low-Income Group has increased substantially from 2.89 million to 7.41 million during the same period (Table 26).

One possible reason could be that the banks are less active in providing housing loan of small amount between ₹ 2 lakh and ₹ 10 lakh. Evidently, the loan volume of ₹ 10 lakh–₹ 25 lakh and above ₹ 25 lakh constitutes the major portion of the housing loan disbursed (Figure 4). Additionally, maximum portion of total outstanding housing loan is in the slab ₹ 5 lakh–₹ 10 lakh and ₹ 10 lakh–₹ 25 lakh (Figure 5). As it has already been mentioned, it is the experiences of the banks that there is an inverse relationship between the NPA (Non-Performing Asset) percentage and the amount of loan with NPA percentage increases with a decrease in size of loan. Evidently, NPA level is highest in case of small size of loan i.e. below ₹ 2 lakh and ₹ 5 lakh and lowest in case of loan exceeding ₹ 25 lakh (Figure 6). Chronic shortage of urban housing not only increases the possibilities of speculation but also allows the unethical practices to perpetuate in urban housing market. More often than not, the consumers tend to ignore the market-irregularities unless otherwise compelled. It is argued that deception in everyday life situation has become so 'widespread and deep that the society instead of complaining and fighting for it has started accepting it' (Bana, 2006: 3). As it has been elaborated later, an effort to understand the consumers' vulnerability and choices vis-à-vis the unethical practices in urban housing market reveals that the consumers frequent a series of tricky practices which are neither avoidable nor acceptable to them. The number of 'registered disputes' does not actually reveal the magnitude of close encounters with such practices since these tricky practices do not always mature as 'dispute' requiring formal institutional intervention. Chronic shortage of urban housing reinforced by limited success of the state in containing the unethical business practices in housing market allow such practices to survive to deny consumer justice (Mukhopadhyay, 2014). What is to be done?

Table 26

Comparative Estimated Shortage of Urban Housing by Economic Groups (2007 and 2012)

Economic Groups	*Year Estimated Shortage in Millions (%)**	
	2007	*2012*
Economically Weaker Section (EWS)	21.78 (88.14)	10.55 (56.18)
Low Income Group (LIG)	2.89 (11.69)	7.41 (39.44)
Middle Income Group and High Income Group (MIG and HIG)	0.04 (0.16)	0.82 (4.38)
Total Housing Shortage	24.71 (100.00)	18.78 (100.00)

* Data within bracket refer to percentage of total.

Source: Report of the Technical Group on Estimation of Housing Shortage (2007–12), GOI, Ministry of Housing and Urban Poverty Alleviation; and Report of the Technical Group on Urban Housing Shortage (TG–12)' (2012–17), GOI. Ministry of Housing and Urban Poverty Alleviation.

Figure 3

Comparative Estimated Shortage of Urban Housing by Economic Groups (2007 and 2012) in Millions (%)

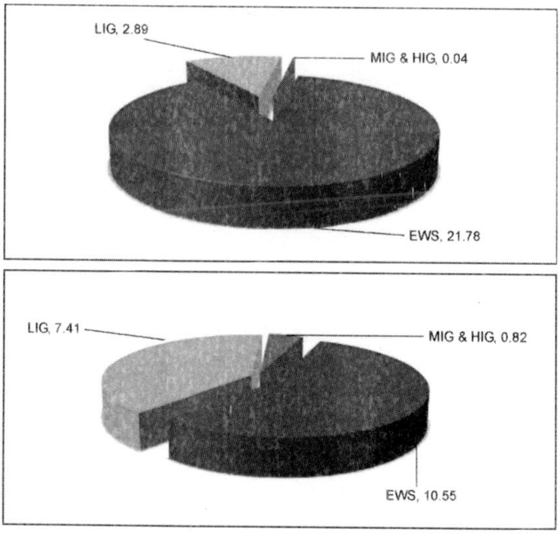

Source: 'Report of the Technical Group on Estimation of Housing Shortage (2007–12)', GOI, Ministry of Housing and Urban Poverty Alleviation; and 'Report of the Technical Group on Urban Housing Shortage (TG–12)' (2012 17), GOI. Ministry of Housing and Urban Poverty Alleviation.

Table 27

Comparative State of Urban Housing Occupied by Households (2007and 2012)

Category of Household	*Year (in Millions)*	
	2007	*2012*
Households (HH) living in non-serviceable Kutcha Houses	2.3	0.99
HH living in Obsolescent Houses	2.39	2.27
HH living in Congested Houses requiring New Houses	12.67	14.99
HH living in Homeless Condition	–	0.53
Total Estimated Shortage	24.71	18.78

Source: 'Report of the Technical Group on Estimation of Housing Shortage (2007–12)'; GOI. Ministry of Housing and Urban Poverty Alleviation; and 'Report of the Technical Group on Urban Housing Shortage (TG-12) (2012–17)'; GOI. Ministry of Housing and Urban Poverty Alleviation,

Figure 4

*Disbursement of Housing Loans**
*FY 2009–10–2011–12 (₹ In Crore)**

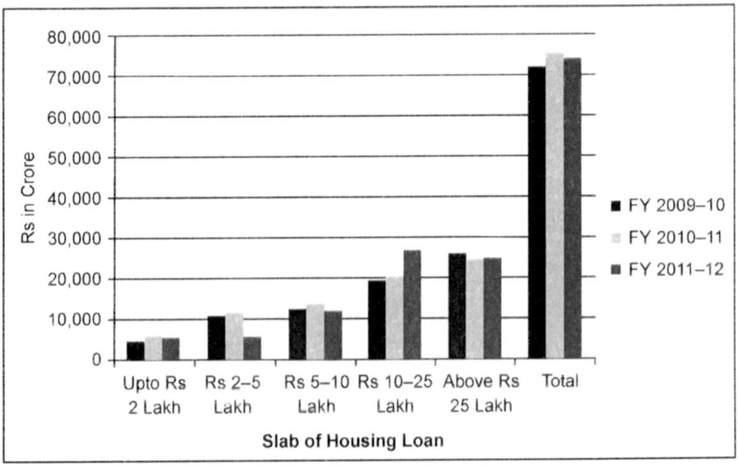

* Public Sector Banks.

Source: Report on Trend and Progress of Housing in India (2012). National Housing Bank, p. 160.

Figure 5

Housing Loan Outstanding
*FY 2009–10 – 2011–12 (₹ in Crore)**

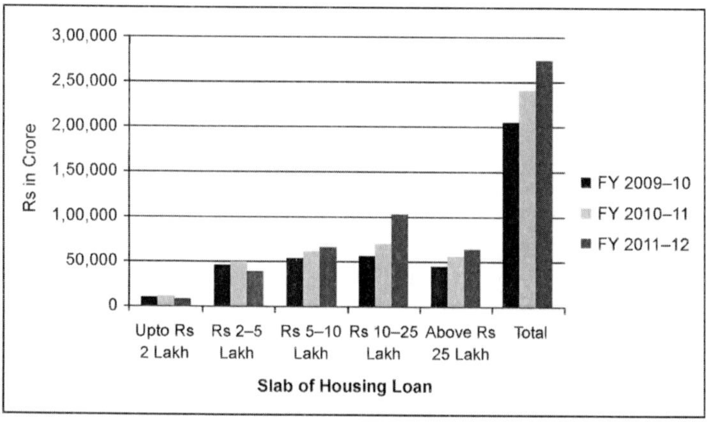

* Public Sector Banks.

Source: Report on Trend and Progress of Housing in India (2012) National Housing Bank, p. 161.

Figure 6

Performance of Loans as per Non-Performing Assets (%)

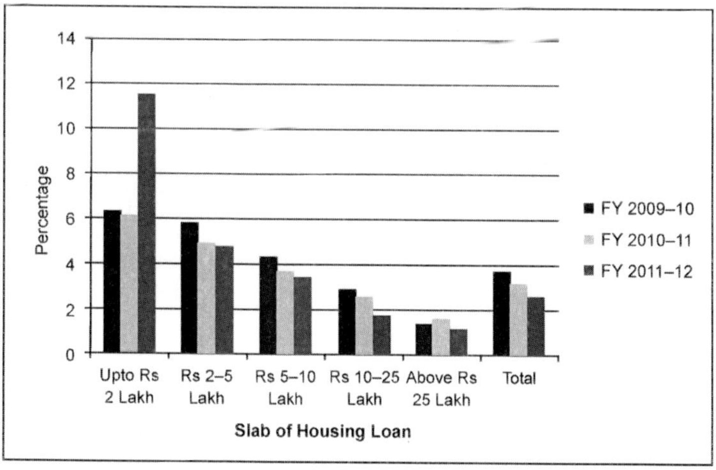

Source: Report on Trend and Progress of Housing in India (2012) National Housing Bank, p. 162.

It is necessary that sufficient reciprocity, in concern for the national agenda i.e. 'Affordable Housing For All', is developed and maintained among the stakeholders. The housing finance companies, whose number is on the rise both in public and private sector, may improvise ways to become more supportive to the home-buyers belonging to the lower end of income distribution in particular. Again, some relaxation in the conditions of the current FDI policy (like the minimum land area, the capitalization and the lock-in period) with respect to the housing and infrastructure sector may attract more investment with necessary implications for the Affordable Housing segment. Also, a regulatory authority is essential to make the housing market more transparent and accountable. When violations of building rules are permitted to be legalized, or, the amount of fine imposed against violation is too small, compared to profit made out of such violation, violation tend to become institutionalized. In Kolkata alone, according to one estimate, about 3,000 cases of unauthorized constructions are legalized annually. The incidence of deception is likely to be high in a market which is speculative, exploitative, non-transparent and unregulated. Undeniably, the state enjoys the legitimacy to pre-empt the deceptive market practices. Shortage of housing is not exclusive of those who are at the lower-end of income distribution. Shortage of housing has been increasing for the MIG and HIG, as well. This has been happening in a situation when the number of unsold under-construction and ready-to-possession residential properties is on the rise particularly in the metros and chiefly because prices of those properties are higher than the budget of the prospective home-buyers. The less resourceful prospective home-buyers are being gradually priced out to the city-fringes/suburbs, the relatively cheaper residential areas with inadequate facilities for basic services. Consequently, the cities are shrinking and the city-fringes/suburbs are growing. While the city-fringes/suburbs are witnessing unplanned growth, a sizeable majority is being eventually denied 'the right to city'.

Notes

1. Kolkata had witnessed slums before it experienced industrial transformation. There are slums which are as old as 150 years. The migrant rural poor, who were absorbed as domestic servants for the British settlers and the Bengali 'babus', were the first group of

dwellers in slums. (Dutta, 2008: 32; Kundu, 2003: 6). They settled in small slums within the English town, 'or how else could the rich get servants, cooks, darwans, chowkidars. cleaners, gardeners, dhobis and the rest?' (Chakravorty, 2000: 65). Their dwellings could even be seen *'within the walking distance of most posh areas of the city'* (Kundu, 2003: 7). With the emergence of new industries in the middle of the nineteenth century, the slum population increased enormously as rural migrants flocked to Kolkata to join work in 'the engineering units and jute and textile mills that began west of the river ... and to work for large transportation projects' (Chakravorty, 2000: 66). The war-induced industrial activities started significantly in the 1930s and 1940s in and around Kolkata and this further led to the migration of cheap labour from the hinterland. These people found cheap accommodation, mostly in huts made of mud and bamboo .... The production of huts without basic infrastructural facilities eventually led to the growth of slums in certain parts of the city (Kundu, 2003: 7). As Kundu (2003: 4) suggests, there are four types of authorized slums in Kolkata. The first kind of slums emerged in colonial period when middlemen built hut type of settlements (on land taken from landowners usually for a long term) to let out to rural migrants. The second variety is 'thika tenant slums' where the slum dwellers have taken possession at a fixed rent and have constructed their own houses. The third type of slums had been constructed by the 'zamindars' (the land lords) themselves to let out to the slum dwellers. The fourth type of slums is Refugee Resettlement Colonies which developed on land available on lease for 99 years (Kundu, 2003: 5). A few words with respect to slums in post-colonial India may be useful.

The Slum Areas (Improvement and Clearance) Act, 1956, defines a slum as 'residential areas where dwellings are unfit for human habitation' because they are dilapidated, cramped, poorly ventilated, unclean or 'any combination of these factors which are detrimental to the safety and health' (Slum Act: 1956). The Committee, constituted 'to look into various aspects of Slum Statistics/Census and issues regarding the conduct of slum Census in 2011' under the chairmanship of Dr Pranab Sen, defines a slum as 'a compact settlement of at least 20 households with a collection of poorly built tenements, mostly of temporary nature, crowded together usually with inadequate sanitary and drinking water facilities in unhygienic conditions'. The new definition of slum is different from the definition adopted by the 2001 Census of India (Slum, 2010: 2–7). The Census on Slum (2011) suggests that the estimated total slum households is 137.5 lakhs which constitutes 17.4 per cent of total urban households of all states and Union Territories (Slum, 2013: 41). The Census data point out that a large section of the urban population in the four metropolitan cities lives in slums with as high as 41.3 per cent in Greater Mumbai, 29.6 per cent in Kolkata, 28 per cent in Chennai and about 15 per cent in Delhi. The Census on Slum (2011) designated slums in three different ways – Notified, Recognized and Identified. Out of 137.49 lakhs of total slum households, 49.65 lakhs households (36.1%) lived in notified slums, 37.96 lakhs (27.6%) lived in recognized slums and 49.88 lakhs (36.3%) lived in identified slums (Slum, 2013: 44). It is important to note that the identified slums, which do not have legal status, have the largest sub-set of slum population, indicating that large number of slums does not have official status as a slum, or access to legal protection and municipal services' (Hindu, 2013). It needs to be noted that the Census office and the National Sample Survey Organization, two government agencies, differ on estimates of India's slum population (*TOI*, 2014; *Frontline*, 2014).

India, after Independence, viewed that slums are 'a disgrace to the country ... a national problem ... it is better to pay for the cost of clearing slums than to continue to pay the mounting cost of slums and suffer destructive effects upon human lives and property indefinitely' (First Five Year Plan). The Slum Areas (Improvement and Clearance) Act, enacted in 1956, provided a definition of 'slum'. Policies have been adopted and budgetary allocation has been made in successive Five Year Plans to 'prevent the growth of slums and tackle the problem of existing slums' in large cities in particular. Without going into details, as some scholars have recently elaborated on slum policy in successive Five Year Plans (Batra: 2009; Chandrasekhar and Mukhopadhyay: 2011, for example), it may be said, between 1956 and 2011 [the passage of the Slum Areas (Improvement and Clearance) Act, 1956, and the announcement of building a slum-free India in 2011], efforts have been made to restrict growth of new slums and to tackle the problems of existing slums through adoption of policies like clearance and improvement of existing slums, environmental improvement of slum areas and extension of affordable urban services to slum dwellers. Ultimately, in 2011, in order to 'encourage the states and the Union Territories to tackle the problem of slums in a definitive manner', Rajiv Awas Yojana (RAY) was announced (for the slum dwellers and the urban poor) with the stated goal of a 'slum-free India' (RAY, 2012: 1). The scheme is claimed to be 'a bold new vision and a new direction to policy, viz., a slum-free India, in which those who live in slums are enabled to aspire for formal acceptance in urban areas by the assignment of property rights to them over their dwelling space' (RAY: 2012a: 1). The available authoritative reports on proliferation of slums and urban housing shortage (2012–17) for the Economically Weaker Section and Low Income Group suggest that more has to be done for a slum-free India. Initiatives appear to be somewhat fractured, often ambivalent, interfered by limitation of resources and commensurate political will. Efforts should be made to reconcile the 'technocratic' vision and the 'democratic' vision of urban development. 'It is no wonder', Batra argues, 'that the sections who have greeted the JNNURM and other urban reform initiatives with such thunderous applause are the corporate media, the real estate lobby, foreign investors, national and international finance capital, international bodies like the WB, the ADB, etc. and middle class citizens' groups' (Batra, 2009: 39).

2. Administrative Report of the Calcutta Municipality, 1872, p. 5 (as quoted in Beattie, Martin (2003), 'Colonial Space: Health and Modernity in Burrabazzar, Kolkata', TDSR, Vol. XIV, NO. II, P.12) http://iaste.berkeley.edu/pdfs/14.2b-Spr03beattie-sml.pdf
3. Administrative Report of the Calcutta Municipality, 1872, p. 6 (as quoted in Beattie, Martin (2003), 'Colonial Space: Health and Modernity in Burrabazzar, Kolkata', TDSR, Vol. XIV, NO. II, P.12) http://iaste.berkeley.edu/pdfs/14.2b-Spr03beattie-sml.pdf
4. The term 'urban poor', for the present purpose, refers to the Economically Weaker Section and the Low Income Group. The household income ceiling of the Economically Weaker Section and the Low Income Group has been revised (vide letter dated 14 November 2012 of the Ministry of Housing and Urban Poverty Alleviation, GOI) as follows:

Economically Weaker Section	:	₹ 1,00,000 per annum (household income)
Low Income Group	:	₹ 1,00,000 to ₹ 2, 00,000 per annum (household income)

The nomenclature of housing units for different income groups (EWS, LIG and MIG) followed is stated below:

Economically Weaker Section (EWS)	:	300 sq ft (Super-built Area)
Low Income Group (LIG)	:	500 sq ft (Super-built area)
Middle Income Group (MIG)	:	600–1,200 sq ft (Super-built Area)

The dwelling units will be provided at costs that permit repayment of home loan in monthly installments not exceeding 30 per cent to 40 per cent of the monthly income of the buyer. (See, Ministry of Housing and Urban Poverty Alleviation, GOI; Report on Trend and Progress of Housing in India–2012 (p. 123), National Housing Bank).

5. The list of companies is available at www.wbhousingboard.in/home/joint_venture_companies (Viewed on 15 May 2014)

The West Bengal Housing Board has recently (14 April 2014) appointed M/S Ernst and Young Pvt. Ltd. as a transaction advisor to make a 'study to draw future modalities in respect of Joint Sector Companies with the West Bengal Housing Board', at http://www.wbhousingboard.in/home/download/correspondance.pdf (Viewed on 12 June 2014)

6. For details, see 'Guidelines for Affordable Housing in Partnership', Ministry of Housing and Urban Poverty Alleviation, GOI, New Delhi www.mhupa.gov.in/w.new/affordablehousing.pdf

   The amended version of the scheme came into effect from 3 June 2011. Available at www.mhupa.gov.in/programs/ahp.htm

   Attention should be drawn to the fact that a Task Force on Affordable Housing was set up in 2008 by the Government of India to define Affordability, suggest financial instruments and other measures to meet the requirement of housing. The Task Force defined affordable house (for various economic groups) in terms of size of dwelling unit and affordability (household income). Accordingly, the carpet area of an affordable house for EWS shall range between 300 and 600 sq. ft. at costs not exceeding four times the household gross annual income and that permit repayment in monthly installments not exceeding 30 per cent of gross monthly income of the buyer. The carpet area of an affordable house for MIG shall not exceed 1,200 sq. ft. and at cost not exceeding five times the household gross annual income and that permit repayment in monthly installments not exceeding 40 per cent of gross monthly income of the buyer (MHUPA 2008). The scheme 'Affordable Housing in Partnership' (2009) amended the definition of affordable housing for various economic groups. As mentioned in the Guidelines for Affordable Housing in Partnership, the affordable houses, for the purpose of this scheme, may be taken as houses ranging from about 300 square feet (super built up area) for EWS, 500 square feet for LIG and 600 square feet to 1,200 square feet for MIG, at costs that permit repayment of home loans in monthly installments not exceeding 30 per cent to 40 per cent of the monthly income of the buyer. In terms of carpet area, EWS category house would be taken as having a minimum 25 sq. mts. of carpet area and the carpet area of an LIG category house would be limited to a maximum of 48 sq. mts. The carpet area of an MIG house would be limited to a maximum of 80 sq. mts.' (MHUPA, 2009). A modified version of the Guidelines for Affordable Housing in Partnership 2009 was released in 2011. The modified version of the scheme made no changes in the definition of affordable housing excepting an addition that 'the size of the rental housing units and dormitories are to be decided by the states based on the needs and requirements of the target segments' (MHUPA, 2011). In supersession of the Guidelines

for Affordable Housing in Partnership issued in 2009, the Ministry of Housing and Urban Development, GOI announced in 2013 that the scheme 'Affordable Housing in Partnership' will continue for the period 2013–22 as part of Rajiv Awas Yojana (MHUPA, 2013). The criterion of minimum carpet area of affordable housing has been modified. Some of the major components are: A. While the carpet area of dwelling units for EWS category will be between 21 sq. mts. and 27 sq. mts., the carpet area of dwelling units for LIG category will be between 28 sq. mts. and 60 sq. mts.; B. The beneficiaries of the housing scheme will be categorized based on annual household income. The annual household income of the EWS category will be up to ₹ 1 lakh. The annual household income of the LIG category will be between ₹ 1 lakh and
₹ 2 lakh; C. Housing projects can have a mix of EWS/LIG/Higher Category dwelling units and commercial units.

The major factors responsible for housing shortage in low income segment are: limited public resources and marginal participation of the private enterprise. The supply-side constraints are: high risk-low profit business; land scarcity and skyrocketing land price; housing finance not available at low interest rate; incentives not sufficient and, Building Approval Process is uncertain adding up to the overhead costs. The demand-side constraints are: high interest rates making the housing finance unaffordable; bank's hesitation to lend to the informal sector employees-non availability of credit and, lack of awareness among the prospective beneficiaries (MHUPA, 2013b).

References

Annual Report (2012): Annual Report (2012–13): *Annual Report,* Ministry of Urban Housing and Poverty Alleviation, Government of India, 79–88.

Bana, Ravinder (2006): 'Housing and Consumer', *Consumer Education Monograph Series,* Indian Institute of Public Administration, New Delhi.

Batra, Lalit (2009): 'A Review of Urbanization and Urban Policy in Post-Independent India', *Working Paper Series,* Centre for the Study of Law and Governance, Jawaharlal Nehru University.

Bettie, Martin (2003): 'Colonial Space: Health and Modernity in Barabazzar, Kolkata; TDSR, Vol. 14, No. 2, pp. 7–20.

Bogle, Linton, J.M. (1929): *Town Planning in India,* Oxford University Press (as quoted in Spodek: 2013).

Bose, Pradip Kumar (2010): 'Refugee, Memory and the State: A Review of Research in Refugee Studies', *Refugee Watch,* Vol. 36, 1 December.

Chakravorty, Sanjoy (2000): 'From Colonial City to Globalizing City: The Far-from Complete Spatial Transformation of Calcutta' in *Globalizing Cities: A New Spatial Order*, Peter Marcuse and Ronald Van Kempen (ed.), Blackwell Publishers, Oxford, pp. 56–77.

Chandrasekhar S. and Mukhopadhyay, Abhiroop (2011): 'Slums: View from successive Five Year Plans', *CPR Urban Brief*, 2 July.

Dutta, Krishna (2008): *Calcutta: A Cultural History*, Northampton, MA: Interlink Books, p. 32; (as quoted in Schenk, Collin W (2010): 'Slum Diversity in Kolkata', *The Columbia Undergraduate Journal of South Asian Studies*, Vol. I, Issue II, P.93–94), pp. 91–108.

Dwivedi, R.M. (2007): *Urban Development and Housing in India*, New Century, New Delhi, (as cited in Batra, Lalit (2009)).

Frontline (2014): 'Slums: Two Stories', *Frontline*, 24 January. http://www.frontline.in/multimedia/archive/01713/Slums_in_India_1713589a.pdf

Gooptu, Nandini (2001): *The Politics of the Urban Poor in Early Twentieth Century India*, Cambridge University Press, Cambridge.

Harrisson, Mark (1994): Anglo-Indian Preventive Medicine 1859–1914, Cambridge University Press, Cambridge.

The Hindu (2013): 'Slum population up, from 52 million to 65 million', 1 October. http://www.thehindu.com/news/national/slum-population-up-from–52-million-to–65-million/article5187166.ece

ICA (2012): Profiles of a Movement: Cooperative Housing Around the World (Geneva, CECODHAS Housing Europe and ICA Housing). www.nabco.ie/_fileupload/Profiles%20of%20a%20movement.pdf

Kidambi, Prashant (2007): *The Making of an Indian Metropolis: Colonial Governance and Public Culture in Bombay, 1890–1920*, Ashgate, England (as quoted in Spodek: 2013)

Kundu, Netai (2003): 'Understanding Slums: Case Studies for the Global Report on Human Settlements', *Urban Slums Reports, The Case of Kolkata*, UN-Habitat, Development Planning Unit, University College London. http://www.ucl.ac.uk/dpu-projects/Global_Report/pdfs/Kolkata_bw.pdf

La Salle, Jones Lang (2012): 'Urban Housing Shortage Rising in India', *Times of India*, Chennai Edition, 5 July.

MHADA (2014): Maharashtra Housing and Area Development Authority. https://mhada.maharashtra.gov.in/?q=history

MHUPA (2008): Report of the High Level Task Force on Affordable Housing For All, GOI Ministry of Housing and Urban Poverty Alleviation. www.naredco.in/pdfs/report-high-level-task.pdf

MHUPA (2009): Guidelines for Affordable Housing in Partnership, GOI Ministry of Housing and Urban Poverty Alleviation (JNNURM Mission Directorate).

MHUPA (2011): Scheme of Affordable Housing in Partnership. GOI Ministry of Housing and Urban Poverty Alleviation (HUDCO and RAY).

MHUPA (2013): Affordable Housing in Partnership-Scheme Guidelines, GOI Ministry of Housing and Urban Poverty Alleviation.

MHUPA (2013b): National Symposium on Affordable Housing, Vigyan Bhawan, New Delhi, 22 July, GOI Ministry of Housing and Urban Poverty Alleviation.

Ministry (2007): Policies and Schemes, Ministry of Housing and Urban Poverty Alleviationh.
ttp://mhupa.gov.in/policies/index2.htm

Mukhopadhyay, Asish (2005): 'Colonial State, Capital, Labour and Industrialization: Coal Mining and Coal Miners in Colonial India, 1919–39', *The Indian Journal of Labour Economics*, Vol. 48, No. 4, October–December, pp. 1015–27.

Mukhopadhyay, Asish (2014): 'Negotiating Unethical Business Practices: Consumers in Urban Housing Market', *International Journal of Business Ethics in Developing Societies*, Vol. 3, No. 1, pp. 1–7.

NCHF (2012): National Cooperative Housing Federation of India, viewed on 12 June 2014.
http://mhupa.gov.in/ministry/associates/autonomousbodies/nchfi.htm

NHBa (2012): Urban Housing, Housing under five years Plans, National Housing Bank, Reserve Bank of India, GOI.
http://www.nhb. org.in/Urban_Housing/5year_plan.php

NHBb, (2012): Report on Trend and Progress of Housing in India, GOI. National Housing Bank, Reserve Bank of India.
http://nhb.org.in/Publications/Report-Trend-and-Progress-of-Housing-in-India–2012.pdf

NHB, (2013): Report on Trend and Progress of Housing in India, GOI. National Housing Bank, Reserve Bank of India.
www.nhb.org.in/Whats_new/Report-on-Trend-and-Progress-of-Housing-in-India–2013.pdf

NUHHP (2007): National Urban Housing and Habitat Policy, Government of India, Ministry of Housing and Urban Poverty Alleviation, New Delhi.

Phatak, Vidyadhar K. (2011): 'Unleashing Urbanization: Urban Planning in India's New Development Strategy', *The India Economy Review*, 15 May.

Ranganathan, Swati (2011): 'Shaping Vibrant Indian Cities', *Business Standard India*–2011, pp. 155–79.

Rangarajan, C. (2001): 'BoP Crisis of 1990–91: Overcoming the Forex Constraint', *Financial Express*, 2 July.

Rao, P.S.N. (2004): 'Transformation of Housing Policies in India-Trend Towards Market Mechanisms'.
https://www.housingauthority. gov.hk/hdw/ihc/pdf/rhk.pdf

RAY (2012): Rajiv Awas Yojana: Guidelines for Slum-free City Planning, Ministry of Housing and Urban Poverty Alleviation, GOI.
http://mhupa.gov.in/w_new/RAY%20Guidelines-%20English.pdf

RAY (2012a): Rajiv Awas Yojana ... Towards a Slum-free India, Guidelines Ministry of Housing and Urban Poverty Alleviation, GOI (see, Preamble, p. 1).

RBI (2009): India's Financial Sector: An Assessment, GOI. Reserve Bank of India, Committee on Financial Sector Assessment, Vol. 2. pp. 191–92.
www.rbi.org.in/scripts/PublicationReportDetails.aspx?UrlPage=&ID=544#VOL2LNK3.5

Real Estate, (2012): Real Estate Sector: Report of the Committee on National Competition Policy, GOI Ministry of Corporate Affairs.
www.iica.in/images/Real Estate Sector.pdf

7th Plan (1985): Seventh Five Year Plan (1985–90), GOI. Planning Commission.
http://planningcommission.nic.in/plans/planrel/fiveyr/7th/vol2/7v2ch12.html

Slum (2010): Report of the Committee on Slum Statistics/Census, Ministry of Housing and Urban Poverty Alleviation, National Buildings Association, New Delhi.

Slum (2013): State of Slums in India: A Statistical Compendium, Ministry of Housing and Urban Poverty Alleviation, National Buildings Association, New Delhi.

Slum Act (1956): The Slum Areas (Improvement and Clearance) Act, 1956

Spodek, Howard (2013): 'City Planning in India under British Rule', *Economic and Political Weekly*, 48 (4), pp. 53–8.

TG-2007–12: Report of the Technical Group on Estimation of Housing shortage (2007–12), GOI Ministry of Housing and Urban Poverty Alleviation.
http://mhupa.gov.in/ministry/housing/HOUSINGSHORTAGE-REPT.pdf

TG-2012–2017: Report of the Technical Group on Urban Housing Shortage (TG-12) (2012–17), GOI Ministry of Housing and Urban Poverty Alleviation.
www.nbo.nic.in/Images/PDF/urban-housingshortage.pdf

TOI (2014): 'Census, NSSO differ on slum population figures', 5 January.
http://timesofindia.indiatimes.com/india/Census-NSSO-differ-on-slum-population-figures/articleshow/28415537.cms

UN-HABITAT (2008): UN-HABITAT (2008): *Housing Finance Mechanism in India* (Nairobi, UN_HABITAT)

CHAPTER 3

Consumerism in India

Evolution and Recent Trends

Consumerism, understood as the initiatives to protect the consumers against fraudulent business practices, is neither a new phenomenon nor has it evolved in India in the recent past. In spite of various legal and non-legislative initiatives, the level of awareness among the consumers about their rights and obligations 'still demands serious attention'. Consumerism in India is plagued by uneven reciprocity among the stakeholders in concern for unfair business practices.

Introduction

The term 'consumerism' refers to the initiatives to protect the consumers against fraudulent business practices. Consumerism, thus defined, is neither a new phenomenon nor has it evolved in India in the recent past. The ancient India had no less concern for the protection of the consumers against unfair practices in business. The capital has become more organized, mobile and aggressive than ever before for a greater share of the emerging markets, posing newer challenges to the consumers and 'consumerism'. The market takes advantage of both: the ignorance and/or reluctance of the consumers to fight the deceptive tendencies in the market and the lapses of the competent authority in terms of rigid enforcement of the rules to curb unfair trade practices. The state's occasional fraudulent practices as an entrepreneur tends to further weaken its position as the regulator of market-irregularities. In globalizing Indian society, the state and the organization of the consumers are engaged in 'critical collaboration' in ensuring consumer justice in a rapidly changing world of consumption. Consumerism in India is, however, plagued by uneven reciprocity among the stakeholders in concern for unfair business practices.

The role of the state to ensure fair business practices has always been crucial, everywhere. The Indian society has had remained alert to the need of initiating measures for the protection of the consumers against fraudulent business practices. Ancient India used to frequent adulteration, imperfect weight and measure and such other unethical business practices. There were rules to regulate such practices. The consumers in British India witnessed enactment of certain crucial laws to prevent unlawful and unethical business practices. The Sale of Goods Act (1930) was the major protective law until the passage of the Consumer Protection Act, 1986. The Consumer Protection Act, 1986 had been enacted with the intention to deliver justice in less formal and at less cost and time. Inarguably, the Act of 1986 has ushered in an era of hope for the consumers with positive implications for the consumer movement in contemporary India.

The consumer movement often called, 'new social movement' or, 'new age movement', has become 'a site of 'critical collaboration' between the state and the non-state organizations of the consumers'. It is possible that 'the identical primary interest of the state and the non-state organizations of the consumers i.e. to effectively reduce the persisting imbalance in the relationship between the buyer and the seller in an imperfect market situation' prevents disintegration. A critical review of the role of the state, as the patron of consumerism, reveals that the state becomes the subject of frequent criticism as an entrepreneur of its own product and services. This encourages one to view the state as both: a patron of consumerism and an occasional fraudulent entrepreneur. The duality of the state vis-à-vis the legitimate interest of the consumers is often overlooked or, overshadowed. But this obviously interferes with the efforts of the state towards effective enforcement of the consumer laws. The efforts of the state tend to become limited or fractured. It is highly probable that the fractured or the limited efforts of the state in protecting the 'rights' of the consumers have facilitated the non-state actors (including the voluntary consumer organizations) to emerge both as a 'critique and a collaborator' to the initiatives of the state for the welfare of the consumers.

This chapter has been divided into four small segments. While Section I deals with the efforts to prevent the fraudulent business practices in India (prior to independence), Section II concerns the legislative as well as the non-legislative initiatives of the state to protect the consumers against unethical business practices in independent India. Section III reflects on the growth of the non-state consumer organizations, the role which these organizations undertake and the major challenges which these organizations encounter and experience in course of role-performance. Section IV is an effort to critically understand the state of the consumers in contemporary Indian society. Also, the outcome of the initiatives of the state and those of the non-state consumer organizations against fraudulent business practices will be touched upon with strategies for strengthening consumerism.

Consumerism in Pre-Independent India

The term 'consumerism' refers to the Acts, Laws, Rules and all such other legal and extra-legal initiatives intended to protect the 'consumers'[1] against actual and potential fraudulent business practices. Consumerism refers to an all-encompassing term, meaning 'nothing more than the consumers' legitimate concern for better value for their money' (Singh and Chadah: 6). The initiatives are not intended to disrupt business activities but to ensure ethics in business. The thrust of consumerism has always been on the development of 'collective consciousness on the part of consumers, business, government and civil society' with the goal to build an environment for fair business practices to the advantage of both. the business and the consumer. Consumerism or initiatives for consumer protection/welfare is neither a new phenomenon nor has it evolved in India in the recent past. It is very likely that initiatives to protect the consumers are as old as the deceptive behaviour of the market. Again, consumerism has not evolved in India only in the recent past. As it has been elaborated in the following paragraphs, Indian society has a long tradition in so far as the protection of the consumers against fraudulent market practices is concerned. The mechanism to protect the consumers against unfair trade practices had been introduced in ancient India. The British India witnessed enactment of crucial protective legal measures. India post-Independence repealed, replaced, amended and enacted Acts including the comprehensive Consumer Protection Act, 1986. Besides, a host of effective extra-legal or, non-legislative measures have been designed to 'socialize' the consumers. It is undeniable that consumerism has assumed greater significance in recent times due to changing social conditions.

Consumerism in Ancient India

In ancient India, adulteration, imperfect weight and measure, sale and purchase of marketable goods at unauthorized prices were no less frequent. To regulate these fraudulent practices, there were rules along with provision of penalty or, punishment. The provisions of penalty or, punishment would undoubtedly ensure greater compliance to those rules. These have references to *Manu Smriti*, the most authentic and oft-quoted text of ancient times, authored by Manu, the ancient law giver.[2] The regulatory measures were indicative of sincere efforts on the part of the rulers to protect the consumers against such possible exploitation in the market. The legal system devoted to consumer welfare of our time had its roots in the identification of the basic issues in consumer welfare in ancient India. Kautilya, in his *Arthashastra*, touched upon many such crucial issues including the issue of consumer protection. Kautilya sincerely believed that 'in the happiness of his subjects lies the king's happiness; in their welfare his welfare'. Protecting the interests of the consumers formed an integral aspect of welfare of the subjects. The consumers would be protected through close vigilance by the state officials. The Chief Controller of State Trading would take care of the trade control system. The commodities and products of the countryside were to be sold in designated market or brought to the city after payment of duty. The profit margin of the merchants was fixed (5% in case of locally produced goods and 10% in case of imported goods). The state remained alert to possible fraudulent transactions and unfair pricing of commodities. It was mandatory to buy all balances and weights from the Chief Superintendents of Weights and Measures. However, manipulation in weight and measure, adulteration, cheating by the goldsmiths and silversmiths were some of the common fraudulent practices encountered and experienced by the consumers of the time. Kautilya provided an exhaustive description of methods of cheating and penalty/punishment for each kind of cheat committed by the merchants, artisans, craftsmen and such other service providers. The time to be taken and charges for various kinds of jobs (e.g.; washing/dyeing job, work involving precious metal) were specified. There were provisions for penalty against manipulation 'in weights and measures, palming of precious metals, miscounting, describing an article of lower quality as of superior quality, giving a false shine, showing one product and selling the other and such other wrong doings' (Patil, 2011; Prasad, 2008; Rangarajan, 2010).

Consumerism in Medieval India

The medieval India witnessed continuity in initiatives for the protection of the consumers. The consumers in medieval India used to enjoy protection against exploitation in the market as reform of the market received adequate attention in medieval India and particularly during the reign of Allauddin Khalji (1290–1320 AD). Allauddin Khalji was the first to introduce price control policy in India. Several measures had been taken to check price of the commodities. These included: (i) fixation of price of the commodities (food grain to slaves), (ii) strict action against the hoarders; (iii) strong espionage system; (iv) action on complaints against unfair practices; (v) establishment of the price control department named; *'Diwan-i-Riayasat'* vi) elimination of the middlemen and, vii) public distribution system (when food grain would be in short supply). The much admired policy of price control of Allauddin Khalji however, ended with his demise (Naz, 2010).

Consumerism in British India

The legal system introduced in British India was a unique 'blend of tradition and modernity'. The British laws, rules and institutions had abiding influence upon the Indian legal system. The Indian tradition and custom was, however, not disobeyed. A modern legal system was introduced to co-exist 'with structural features (e.g. a system of separate personal laws) and rules (e.g. *Dharma,* and local custom)' of a traditional legal system. Blending the two legal traditions was indeed a great challenge. The task was successfully accomplished and a 'unified, nationwide, modern legal system' evolved in British India. Such a difficult task could be accomplished largely because 'the law itself underwent considerable adaptation' (Galanter, 1997). In order to protect the interest of the consumers, Acts were enacted in British India. The major Acts, having at least some concern for consumer protection, were: (i) The Indian Penal Code, 1860; (ii) The Sale of Goods Act, 1930; (iii) The Agricultural Produce (Marking and Grading) Act, 1937; (iv) The Drugs and Cosmetics Act, 1940. Each of these Acts is described in brief.

The Indian Penal Code (IPC), 1860, consists of certain provisions which act as insurance to the consumers against potential fraudulent trade practices. Section(s) 264 to 267 of the IPC, 1860, (under Chapter XIII entitled: Offences Relating to Weights and Measures) are concerned with fraudulent use of false instrument of weighing (Section 264); fraudulent use of false weight or measure (Section 265); being in possession of false weight or measure (Section 266); and, making or selling false weight or measure (Section 267). The offenders may be punished with imprisonment for a term extendable up to one year or with fine or with both. Sections 272 to 276 of the IPC, 1860, (under Chapter XIV entitled, Offences affecting the public health, safety, convenience, decency and morals) deal with following offences and punishment for such offences. Section 272 deals with adulteration of food or drink intended for sale and Section 273 deals with sale of noxious food or drink. Sections 274 to 276 deal with offences related to adulteration of drugs (Section 274); sale of adulterated drugs (Section 275); and, sale of drugs as a different drug or preparation (Section 276). These offences are punishable with imprisonment or with fine or with both (IPC, 1860).

The Sale of Goods Act, 1930, as it has already been stated, was the major source of protection to the consumers against unfair trade practices until the passage of the Consumer Protection Act, 1986. In India, until the passage of the Sale of Goods Act 1930, there was the Indian Contract Act, 1872, to govern the sale of goods. The sale of goods in India would actually follow the English Common Law as the Indian Contract Act, 1872, was based on the English Common Law. By 1920, it was strongly felt that some provisions of the Indian Contract Act related to sale of goods required modification in view of 'new developments in mercantile transactions'. As well, given the growing importance of this segment of the Indian Contract Act 1872, a separate Act embodying the provisions pertaining to sale of goods was felt necessary. The Sale of Goods Act came into being in 1930 and the Chapter VII of the Indian Contract Act was repealed. The Sale of Goods Act, 1930, as enacted in India, had its roots in the English Sale of Goods Act of 1893 but 'modified in the light of subsequent judicial decisions in England and India' (Law Commission: 1958). Section 16 of the Sale of Goods Act, 1930, relates to 'implied conditions as to quality or fitness'. Sub-section (1) and Sub-section (2) of the Sale of Goods Act, 1930, relate to implied condition regarding 'fitness for purpose' and 'merchantable quality', respectively. Again, Section 12 of the said Act deals with 'condition and warranty' (SGA, 1930).

The Agricultural Produce (Grading and Marking) Act, 1937, deals with grading and marking of agricultural and other produce. The central government is empowered to 'prescribe compulsory grade designation in respect of certain articles' in public interest or for protection of the consumers. This Act empowers the central government to make rules to implement the provisions of this Act and in particular (i) to fix grade designation to indicate the 'quality' of any 'scheduled article'; (ii) to define the quality indicated by every 'grade designation'; and (iii) to specify 'grade designation marks' to represent particular grade designation.[3] Any 'authorized officer' shall have the power to 'enter any premises at any reasonable time and make necessary inspection of and search for, the agricultural produce in relation which contravention has been or is being made' and 'may seize and detain any agricultural produce in relation to which an offence under this Act appears to have been committed/intended/likely to be used in the commission of such offence'. Unauthorized marking with grade designation mark; counterfeiting grade designation mark and selling mis-graded articles are punishable offences under this Act (APGM, 1937). There is provision for redressal of consumers' grievances and complaints in respect of Agmark graded product. If the complaint is found genuine, the authorized packer or the seller of graded product is directed to make free-of-cost replacement of the product to the complainant within a stipulated time.[4] Where free-of-cost replacement may not be possible for any reason, there is provision for reimbursement of actual price or that of comparable quality and quantity of the produce.[5]

The Drugs and Cosmetics Act, 1940, (amended many times and to subsequently include 'cosmetics' within its fold in 1964), regulates 'import, manufacture, sale and distribution of drugs and cosmetics.[6] The Act regulates misbranded, adulterated and spurious drugs and misbranded and spurious cosmetics in public interest. The provisions of this Act are additional and do not bar the application of the Dangerous Drugs Act, 1930. The Act covers Ayurvedic, Siddha and Unani drugs and necessary provisions for these drugs are included in a separate chapter (IVA). The Act includes provisions on penalties to be imposed for offences and subsequent offences.

Consumerism in Independent India

India, since her Independence, has repealed, replaced and amended certain Acts as well as enacted new Acts for the protection of the consumers under changing conditions. The new Acts include: the Essential Commodities Act, 1955; the Standard of Weight and Measures Act 1976; the Consumer Protection Act, 1986. With the passage of the Food Safety and Standard Act, 2006, some legislation and orders have been repealed and these include: Prevention of Food Adulteration Act, 1954; Fruit Products Order 1955, Meat Food Products Order 1973; Vegetable Oil Products (Regulation) Order 1947; Edible Oil Packaging (Regulation) Order 1998; Solvent Extracted Oil, De-oiled Meal and Edible Flour (control) Order 1967; Milk and Milk Products Order and all other Orders under the Essential Commodities Act 1955 (Patil, 2011). Again, the Bureau of Indian Standard Act, 1986, has replaced the Bureau of Indian Standard (Certification Marks) Act, 1952 (Panta, 2001). Mention should be made that the Consumer Protection Act, 1986, has been amended thrice (1991, 1993 and 2002). Also, further amendment to the Act is under consideration. A few words related to the Consumer Protection Act, 1986, may be useful.

Consumer Protection Act, 1986

The Consumer Protection Act 1986 was passed immediately after the UN endorsed the UN Guidelines on Consumer Protection (UNGCP) in 1985. The Consumer Protection Act, 1986, had been enacted to:

> Provide better protection of the interests of consumers and for that purpose to make provision for the establishment of consumer councils and other authorities for the settlement of consumers' disputes and for matters connected therewith (CPA, 1986).

Why passage of the Consumer Protection Act, 1986, was necessary? Could it be that the Consumer Protection Act, 1986, has become more relevant in the context of rapidly changing world of consumption and world of business in globalizing Indian society?

Arguably, it would be necessary to enact this Act had this Act not been enacted. It is best put in some detail.

First, the world of consumption has been rapidly changing, everywhere. The liberalizing of the economies, the concomitant of economic globalization, has allowed the entrepreneurs to become engaged in desperate quest for market to sell their product and services. Opening up of the economies has not only made availability of goods and services much easier. It has transformed the taste, the preference, the choice, the aspiration, to be precise, the orientation to life and living of the consumers in the liberalizing societies including that of India. With rapid change in the world of consumption and access to goods and services becoming easier than ever before, the chances of being victims of improper choice and fraudulent behaviour of the market has increased manifold;

Second, it is though the world of consumption has been rapidly changing, the market in India is still dominated by the ill-informed and ill-organized consumers. The rural segment of the Indian market has also convincing potentialities for growth with substantial demand for both products and services. The rural India is poised to lead even in Fast Moving Consumer Goods sector and not alone in agri-business. Reports are available to suggest that the consumers are to negotiate varying forms of deception in every-day life from misleading advertisement to medical negligence to 'tricky practices' in housing market;

Third, the world of business has been changing fast. The revolution in Information and Communication Technology has facilitated the market to introduce newer strategies to aggressively promote their products and services through e-commerce and e-business. Though the e-commerce operations are already covered under the Consumer Protection Act, 1986, the state has been planning to further amend the Consumer Protection Act to prevent alleged cheating and malpractices by the companies (*TOI*, 2014). Payment through cash is gradually being substituted by payment through e-cards: credit card, debit card and pre-paid card. As the consumers are being accustomed to e-cards, the Indian economy is in transition – from cash to cashless economy. Between 2008 and 2013, credit card spends (in value terms) have more than doubled to ₹ 1.23 lakh and debit card spends (in value) have increased six times to ₹ 74,400 crore (*TOI*, 2013). It is important to note that a category-wise data on complaints, as presented in the Annual Report on Banking Ombudsman Scheme, suggest that the number of complaints related to credit/debit cards have been steadily increasing from 14,492 in 2011–12 to 18,474 in 2013–14. The complaints related to cards forms the second largest category of complaints (RBI, 2015). The infusion of advanced technology with business has been a newer cause of worries to the consumers;

Fourth, business is becoming impersonal. The personal relationship between the buyer and the seller has been gradually disappearing as the markets are no more physical places where buyers and sellers come in contact with each other (Singh and Chadah: 9; Kapoor: 5). Buying and selling of products and services is increasingly being done through call centres.

Finally, it is for the first time that an Act has provided the definition of a 'consumer'. Again, never before the passage of the Act, the 'consumers' in Indian society would enjoy legal rights including the right to be informed, to be heard and to seek redressal. As well, the provisions of the Act are compensatory in nature. This means that the Act makes provision for due compensation to the victim of unscrupulous behaviour of the market.

Salient Features

At least, a couple of significant provisions of the Act demand particular attention. These are: first; 'save as otherwise expressly provided by the Central Government by notification, this Act shall apply to all goods and services' *[Section 1(4)]* ; second, 'The provisions of this Act shall be in addition to and not in derogation of the provisions of any other law for the time being in force.' (Section 3).

The salient features of the Act, the rights of the consumers as enshrined in the Act and the provision of penalties may be mentioned as follows:

1. The Act provides for establishing a three-tier consumer dispute redressal machinery at the national, state and district levels.
2. The Act applies to all goods and services unless specifically exempted.
3. The Act covers all sectors: private, public or, co-operative.
4. The provisions are compensatory in nature.

5. The Act provides adjudicatory authorities, which are simple, speedy and also less expensive.
6. The Act provides for setting up of Consumer Protection Councils at the central, state and district levels, which are advisory bodies to promote and protect the rights of the consumers.
7. The provisions of the Act are in addition to and not in derogation of the provisions of any other law for the time being in force (Chaddah and Singh; Report, 2012–17).

Rights of Consumers

The Consumer Protection Act, 1986 guarantees a set of six rights to the consumers. These are:

1. The right to be protected against marketing of goods and services which are hazardous to life and property.
2. The right to be informed about the quality, quantity, potency, purity, standard and price of goods or services, as the case may be to protect the consumer against unfair trade practices.
3. The right to be assured, wherever possible to have an access to variety of goods and services at competitive prices.
4. The right to be heard and to be assured that consumers interests will receive due consideration at appropriate forum.
5. The right to seek redressal against unfair trade practices or restrictive trade practices or unscrupulous exploitation of consumers.
6. The right to consumer education (Report, 2012–17: 65).

Penalties

Section 27, Consumer Protection Act, 1986, contains provisions for penalties:

1. Where a trader or a person against whom a complaint is made or the complainant fails or omits to comply with any order made by the District Forum, the State Commission or the National Commission, as the case may be, such trader or person or complainant shall be punishable with imprisonment for a term which shall not be less than one month but which may extend to three years, or with fine which shall not be less than ₹ 2,000 but which may extend to ₹ 10,000, or with both.

2. Notwithstanding anything contained in the Code of Criminal Procedure, 1973, (2 of 1974), the District Forum or the State Commission or the National Commission, as the case may be, shall have the power of a Judicial Magistrate of the first class for the trial of offences under this Act, and on such conferment of powers, the District Forum or the State Commission or the National Commission, as the case may be, on whom the powers are so conferred, shall be deemed to be a Judicial Magistrate of the first class for the purpose of the Code of Criminal Procedure, 1973 (2 of 1974).
3. All offences under this Act may be tried summarily by the District Forum or the State Commission or the National Commission, as the case may be (CPA, 1986).

To be precise, the Consumer Protection Act, 1986, is a benevolent social legislation to ensure less expensive and speedy redressal of the grievances of the consumers. The Act makes it mandatory to establish a three-tier consumer redressal mechanism to ensure consumer justice. It is argued:

> By spelling out the rights and remedies of the consumers in a market so far dominated by organized manufacturers and traders of goods and providers of various types of services, the Act makes the dictum, *caveat emptor* ('buyer beware') a thing of the past (NCDRC).

Also, there are some other legislative initiatives which needs mentioning.[7]

Non-Legislative Measures

Apart from repealing, replacing, enacting and amending laws, a host of non-legislative measures are sponsored by the state to 'socialize' the consumers. The host of state-sponsored awareness programmes includes audio spots and video spots, publication of journal, booklet, cinema slide shows, animation films, advertisement in print and electronic media, organization of training programmes, institution of award. The scheme under the brand name of '*Jago Grahak Jago*' has 'carved out a niche for itself.' The Ministry of Consumer Affairs finances various Voluntary Consumer Organizations for conducting comparative tests of products and services. This helps the consumers to compare the products and take purchase decisions diligently. This allows to protect one of the rights of the consumers as enshrined in the Consumer Protection Act, 1986, that is, the right to choose. Again there is the State Consumer Helpline Knowledge Resource Management Portal (SCHKRMP) located in a good number of states. The advisors at State Consumer Helpline (SCH) provide pre-purchase information, post-purchase advice, guidance and information and also offer 'next-step advice' for resolution or redress. The SCH publishes newsletter, bulletin and issues advisories on regular basis. Efforts are being made through various means to sensitize the consumers of their responsibilities of being: Critically Aware, Involved, Organized, Responsible towards the Environment and Practicing Sustainable Consumption. Also, the institutions of higher learning are encouraged to organize seminars, workshops and pursue sponsored research programmes on issues related to consumer protection. Again, 7,749 Consumer Clubs have been set up in schools/colleges. Also, grants-in-aid are provided to the states and Union Territories to carry out consumer awareness activities.

At the central level, there is the *Department of Consumer Affairs* under the *Ministry of Consumer Affairs, Food and Public Distribution* to prevent possible fraudulent activities through protection of the rights of the consumers and redressal of grievances of the consumers. The National Action Plan has been launched for raising awareness among the consumers and enforcement of the CPA, 1986. Again, there is the *Consumer Welfare Fund* engaged in ensuring providing financial assistance for welfare of the consumers and strengthening the voluntary consumer movement in the country. The *Centre for Consumer Studies (CCS)* at the *Indian Institute of Public Administration (IIPA)* acts as the Nodal Agency of the Department of Consumer Affairs, Ministry of Consumer Affairs, to facilitate in-depth action research in the area of consumer welfare. A few words about the Centre for Consumer Studies may be relevant. The role of the Centre for Consumer Studies is operational as well as promotional. 'It acts as a forum for creating dialogue among policy makers, service providers, representatives of various business establishments and their associations, professional bodies/associations, civil society organization, educational/research institutions, economic and social development organizations as well as leading NGOs. It also acts as a storing and clearing-house for the exchange and constant flow of information, ideas and activities relating to consumer protection and welfare' (CCS, 2014).[8]

Non-State Consumer Organizations: Growth

The Passengers and Traffic Relief Association (PATRA), established in Bombay (now Mumbai), in 1915, was perhaps the first collective initiative towards consumer welfare in India. The Women Graduate Union (WGU), born in the same year, was another organization. Immediately after India's Independence, C. Rajagopalachari, a Gandhian, established the Consumer Protection Council in Madras (now Chennai), in 1949. This gave a formal shape to the consumer movement in India. The activities of the Consumer Protection Council were limited in terms of geographical area. It was confined to the state of Tamil Nadu alone. The desired change, in terms of sustained and visible campaigns and expansion, came only around the 1960s, with the setting up of the Consumer Guidance Society of India (CGSI) and such other organizations (*Business Today*: 2002). The CGSI was founded by the women activists in the year 1966. The aim of the CGSI was to protect the rights of the consumers, who found themselves helpless whenever they were supplied with defective goods or services. The Indian Association of Consumers, established in 1956 (Delhi), made efforts to extend its activities across India but with limited success. Some other organizations emerged in the 1960s. In the 1970s, organizations like Visakha Consumers Council, Akhil Bharatiya Grahak in Pune, Mumbai Grahak Panchayat, Grahak Panchayat in Jamshedpur were established mainly to take care of the wholesale prices and the quality of the product of everyday use. The National Consumer Protection Council, which is primarily engaged in collection of consumer information, assist the state government in the consumer movement, examine consumer grievances, initiate remedial measures and promote equitable distribution, should be located as an important milestone in strengthening the consumer movement in the country. The Indian Consumers' Union was established in 1977 to fight against the spiralling prices of essential commodities. In 1979, the Consumer Education and Research Centre (CERC) came into existence in Ahmedabad (Seetharaman and Sethi: 2002). The Voluntary Organization in the Interest of the Consumer Education (VOICE) was born in 1993 in Delhi. VOICE is a voluntary action group, consisting of academics, professionals and volunteers, committed to creating informed consumers. It is engaged in raising awareness among the consumers not only about malpractices perpetuated in the market place but also about the rights to which a consumer is entitled. The organization publishes a bi-monthly magazine that focuses on bringing consumers information on product performance.[9] In Jaipur, the Consumer Unity and Trust Society (CUTS) came into existence in 1984. Its major activities include spreading awareness among the consumers through publication of books and periodicals and carrying out research on Indian consumers. Again, in 1993, a group of individuals with the common concern for consumer welfare formed the Consumer Coordination Council (Seetharaman and Sethi, 2002; Narayanaswamy, 1999; Verma, 2002). As of now, the Consumer Coordination Council (CCC) has a membership reach of over 84 leading Consumer Organizations, spread over different parts of the country, which are, or have been members of the Central Consumer Protection Council (CCPC), set up under the Consumer Protection Act. The major aims and objectives of CCPC are first, to influence policies, legislation and administrative framework towards promotion of consumer welfare; and second, to empower the consumer protection groups to work towards strengthening the civil society in the democratic system of the country.

There are industrial associations like the Confederation of Indian Industries (CII), Federation of Indian Chambers of Commerce and Industry (FICCI), the Advertisement Standard Council of India (ASCI) and the ASSOCHAM which act as the non-governmental actors for consumer welfare by way of imbibing awareness among the members of their respective organizations, the corporate leaders, on quality of products and services and customer care. Induced by the efforts of these organizations, at least some enterprises (for example, the public sector banks) have decided to meet the customers directly and on regular basis to advise their customers towards resolution of grievances, if any. Also, some companies have become responsive to the grievances of their customers to avoid possible loss of monetary and goodwill resulting from legal action taken by the deceived consumers (Paul, 2010).

In India, the National Consumer Day is celebrated on 15 March, every year. It was on this day in 1962, the Bill for Consumer Rights was moved in the US Congress preceded by reiteration of the

US President John F. Kennedy for total commitment to promotion and protection of consumer interests. It is, however, interesting to note that 15 March is not observed as a special day in US. Inspired by the success of the 'Swadeshi Movement' to boycott foreign cloth, salt etc. CUTS declared and adopted 'the right to resist and boycott any person, goods or services in the event of conflict with consumer's interest' on 15 August 1990. Again, on 26 January 1991, CUTS declared and adopted 'the right to opportunities to acquire basic needs which will enable one to work and to earn a living, without exploitation'. Both these rights were adopted at the Third National Convention of Consumer Activists at Calcutta during 1–3 November 1991(CUTS: 2012).

Consumer International was founded in 1960. With over 240 Member Organizations in 120 countries, Consumer International (CI) is the world federation of consumer groups and 'serves as the only independent and authoritative global voice for consumers'. Consumer International is primarily engaged in building a powerful international movement to help protect and empower consumers everywhere. The organization is committed: (i) to defend, promote, develop and pursue Consumer Rights as the international basis of consumer protection; and (ii) to support, develop and work directly with the constituent member organizations, seeking to protect, inform, give a voice to and secure rights for consumers, worldwide.[10] There are innumerable other non-state organizations including voluntary consumer organizations operating both at national and state level for the protection of the interests of the consumers.

Non-state Consumer Organizations: Role

In India, the non-state consumer organization namely the Passenger and Traffic Relief Association, as stated above, started its journey 100 years ago. Since then the number of non-state consumer organizations including the voluntary consumer organizations has increased manifold. A recent empirical study, carried out on the non-state (including the voluntary) consumer organizations in the state of West Bengal, reveals that these organizations contribute to the promotion of consumerism by way of undertaking four major activities (Paul, 2010). These are: (i) promotion of awareness among the members and significant others about the Acts and Rules protecting the interests of the consumers as well as the rights and obligations of the consumers; (ii) organization of state-sponsored programmes related to consumer welfare; (iii) mobilization of protest against alleged fraudulent practices and; finally, advocacy for resolution of disputes to the members of one's own organization. The study also points to the challenges of the non-state consumer organizations.

Non-State Organizations: Challenges

In India, the non-state consumer organizations, in course of role-performance, face a series of challenges. The major challenges, which these organizations ordinarily experience, are: motivating the consumers, financial constraint and, uneven reciprocity between the state and the non-state consumer organizations. Each of these is put in some detail.

Motivating the Consumers

It is commonplace that motivating an individual to participate in a programme related to consumer welfare is indeed a difficult task. Again, persuading a consumer to seek redressal against fraudulent behaviour turns into a serious challenge for the organization. The victim of fraudulent practices hesitates to recourse to legal path mainly to avoid the 'costs' (money, time and energy) associated with the process of redressal. Again, it is possible that the fraudulent trader is not only known to the victim but also one of his neighbours. In a suburb in particular, people tend to develop primary (face-to-face) relationship with one's neighbour. Formally lodging a complaint by one against the other may result in rupture of social bond and, more so, when the outcome of a legal dispute is unknown. Besides, there is the fear of denial of service from the trader in future.

Crisis of Fund

Financial support, available from the state authority, to run programmes related to consumer welfare are both: inadequate and irregular. Annual subscription of the members and nominal case fee are the other sources of income of these organizations. These hardly leave any surplus for the organizations to organize programmes on their own and on regular basis. Fund crisis tend to limit the activities of these organizations.

Bond of Uneven Reciprocity

Both, the state and the non-state consumer organizations, are committed to the sustenance of consumerism. The difference that persists between these two is more one of approaches than policies. There persists a bond of uneven reciprocity between them. It is the perception of the non-state consumer organizations that the state is not adequately alert to the financial needs of these organizations. The state, on the other hand, expects greater participation of these organizations in implementation of the programmes in line with the directives of the state (Mukhopadhyay and Paul, 2010).

Consumers in Contemporary India

In spite of various legal and non-legislative initiatives of the state for consumer welfare, guaranteed rights of the consumers and introduction of formal redressal mechanism for speedy disposal of disputes, the level of awareness among the consumers in India about the rights and obligations 'still demands serious attention'. It is chiefly ill-information or, mal-information on the part of the consumers about the products and services which they buy from the market that allow them to be deceived in everyday life. The consumers also suffer from lack of adequate knowledge about the simple, speedy and less expensive grievance-redressal mechanism available to the consumers. As well, the consumers are hesitant/reluctant to 'contest' unless otherwise compelled. As it has been elaborated later, these largely explain as to why the unethical practices in the market persist. A recent study (carried out in India by the CUTS Centre for Consumer Action, Research and Training) provides useful clues towards an understanding of the state of the consumers in contemporary India. The study indicates that

1. only 25 per cent of the consumers know about the Consumer Protection Act, 1986;
2. only 42 per cent of the respondents are aware of the rights of the consumers;
3. only 47 per cent are aware of the grievance redressal mechanism;
4. only 28 per cent believe that the common people have access to the redressal mechanism;
5. 93 per cent of the respondents reported that 'they never bothered to lodge a complaint';

6. of the remaining 7 per cent of the respondents, who approached the redressal mechanism, 'only 0.3 per cent have achieved redress' (CUTS, 2012).

It is true that the number of cases filed in various fora and more particularly in District Forum has been increasing over the years (Table 28). However, the observation of the above study that only 7 per cent of the consumers 'bother to lodge complaints formally' suggests that the number of cases formally filed do not actually reveal the magnitude of fraudulent practices encountered and experienced by the consumers in everyday life situation. The reasons, as provided by the study, for poor reporting of cases, are (1) ignorance about the redressal procedure and (2) lack of faith on the redressal procedure. The study has recorded that 53 per cent of the consumers are not familiar with the redressal mechanism. Also, it is believed by a sizeable majority, close to three-fourth (72%), of the respondents that the common people do not have access to the redressal process. This means that the awareness programme are required to be designed not only to make the consumers alert about their rights and but also to erase the misgivings, if any, about the redressal procedure in particular from which the consumers in contemporary India still suffer. It can't be ruled out that the consumers may also have other reasons which dissuade them to file a case in an appropriate forum. More on this will be said later.

Making the consumers in peri-urban and rural India aware of their rights, the protective laws and redressal mechanism is important as the peri-urban and rural India has been experiencing conspicuous changes in world of consumption. As already stated, it is generally agreed upon that future market lies in peri-urban and rural India. Recent trends on pattern of consumption in India suggest that consumption in rural India has been growing at a pace faster than that of urban areas. The trend had been visible in 15 of the 17 major states in India. It is reported, in many states, the gap between urban and rural consumption has closed at a very fast pace. In Bihar, for instance, rural consumption has increased at a CAGR of 17.2 per cent, against 8.2 per cent in urban areas. In Chhattisgarh, rural spending rose at 15.3 per cent (urban 5.6%) and in Odisha at a CAGR of 15.7 per cent (urban 7.8%).[11] It is not alone agri-business, the peri-urban and rural India is also poised to lead in sector like FMCG (Fast Moving Consumer Goods). Recent studies on rural consumers, however, suggest that they are deceived at the

Table 28

Total Number of Consumer Complaints Filed/Disposed Since Inception Under Consumer Protection Law As on 30.06.2011 and 01.08.2014

Name of Agency	*Cases Filed Since Inception*		*Cases Disposed of Since Inception*		*Cases Pending*		*% of Total Disposal*	
	2011	*2014*	*2011*	*2014*	*2011*	*2014*	*2011*	*2014*
National Commission	69,465	89,495	60,504	77,770	8,961	11,725	87.10	86.90
State Commissions	5,41,478	6,45,486	440613	5,54,341	1,00,865	91,145	81.37	85.88
District Fora	29,92,338	34,42,730	27,36,379	31,76,518	2,55,959	2,66,212	91.45	92.27

Source: Report (2012–17): Report of the Working Group on Consumer Protection, Twelfth Plan (2012–17), Vol. II, Department of Consumer Affairs, Ministry of Consumer Affairs, Food and Public Distribution, GOI (for data as on 30 June 2011) p. 49.
National Consumer Disputes Redressal Commission; http://ncdrc.nic.in/ (for data as on 1 August 2014)

market place in various forms; from fake FMCG product (both 'counterfeit' and 'pass-off') to inflated electricity and telephone bill to medical negligence. No wonder that the consumers in peri-urban and rural India suffer from high level of ignorance about their rights and protective consumer laws. The major sources of low level of awareness among them could be found associated with the perennial problems of economic inequality and low level of literacy.

The study, carried out by the Indian Institute of Public Administration, New Delhi, made an attempt to understand the factors responsible for the weak progress of the consumer movement in India. The study had been carried out in five states viz.; Uttar Pradesh, Gujarat, Karnataka, Odisha and Tripura. The said study revealed that 'it's not just people's lack of education of consumer rights but inefficient redressal mechanism and insufficient efforts by government that have made consumer protection movement a failure' (Dash: 2014). The study recorded that over 67 per cent of the respondents were unaware of the laws and only 33 per cent were either aware of the law to large extent or to some extent. The study revealed that there were four major factors responsible for the failure of the Consumer Protection Act. Of these, 'lack of education about rights among the consumers' was found most crucial (75.4%) followed by 'ineffective redressal mechanism' (68.1%) and 'insufficient efforts of the state' (62.3%). The other significant factor responsible recorded: 'traders/business were more powerful (62%).

The Working Group on Consumer Protection (Twelfth Plan, 2012–17) noted that level of awareness among the consumers is low. It is though the level of consumer awareness varies from state to state depending upon the level of literacy and the social awareness of the people. The major reasons for low level of consumer awareness in India, as identified by the Working Group are: (a) vastness of the country, a large population of which is below poverty line; (b) the consumers are not able to assert and protect themselves due to the economic inequality, low level of literacy and ignorance and, therefore, easily get exploited by the trade, industry and service providers. As a remedy, the Working Group has put thrust on, among others, educating the consumers about their rights and responsibilities through a concerted awareness-building programme. A national awareness programme, the sub-group on Consumer Awareness and Education prescribes, requires to be launched 'aggressively at the grassroot level through state government and local VCOs for the benefit of the more vulnerable categories of consumers such as: women and children; youth; farmers and rural families; middle and working class' (Report, 2012–17: 64).[12]

There is no reason to believe that the urban India is well-informed and more aware about the rights of the consumers compared to their rural counterparts. A recent study, undertaken by ASSOCHAM among about 4,000 participants and comprising an equal number of male and female respondents, reveals that about 70 per cent of the urban Indian is still ignorant, complacent and ill-informed about their rights and existing law. Besides promotion of products and services through misleading advertisements in various media together with lack of transparency, complex terms and conditions, non-disclosure of hidden charges/fees, penalties and others are certain key concerns of modern Indian consumers (*Business Line*, 2014).

Outcome of Initiatives

It is least contested that unethical business practices adversely impact economic growth as well as investment opportunities of an economy, apart from the business image of the enterprises engaged in such practices. Unfair business practices pose a challenge to the 'consumers' and 'consumerism', as well. Unless otherwise compelled, the market takes advantage of ignorance and/or reluctance and/or tolerance of the consumers to fight the deceptive tendencies in the market and limited concern of the competent authority in terms of rigid enforcement of the rules to curb unfair trade practices, wherever necessary. The state's occasional fraudulent practices as an entrepreneur tend to further weaken its position as the regulator of market-irregularities.

It is true that the corporate sector has all along been a crucial partner to India's development. It is also true that the corporate sector does not shy away from adopting unfair and corrupt practices. A recent study with respect to Indian economy suggests that 'the potential losses suffered by the Indian economy stands at ₹ 364 billion and this excludes some large scams such as 2G, Commonwealth Games and Mining'. The study is based on cases of corruption reported in media between October 2011 and September 2012 (EY-FICCI, 2012). Again, 'some industries tend to have relatively higher instances of bribery and corruption than others'. This becomes possible chiefly 'because of link with multiple parties including government' (KPMG, 2011). An unmistakable frustration continues to be associated with the performance of the public sector both as a producer and a service provider. And, 'their drift in this direction owes more to ... dispensing patronage and buying out politically the vested interests of the day' (Balkrishnan: 2007). The outcome of the initiatives of the state and the non-state organizations for promotion of consumerism in globalizing India has to be understood in the light of rapidly changing social conditions.

True it is, consequent upon the opening up of the Indian economy; the consumers are enjoying access to a greater variety of products and services than ever before. The chances of being victims of fraudulent business practices have not, however, diminished. The business entrepreneurs, national or multi-national, large or small, are more organized and mobile. In a competitive world of consumption, they are too aggressive in selling their products and services. The rural India is not immune to aggressive selling strategies, either.

The infusion of advanced technology with business has been a newer cause of worries to the consumers. The traditional art of buying and selling has been slowly disappearing. An impersonal form of shopping has been emerging. Buying and selling of product and service is being done through call centres. Cashless transaction, preferably through debit/credit card/net-banking, is being encouraged where it is not mandatory.

The success of a welfare mission depends largely on sufficient concern and co-ordination among the stakeholders. Consumerism in India is plagued by uneven reciprocity in concern for unfair business practices among the stakeholders: the state, the market and the consumers. The state's occasional fraudulent practices as an entrepreneur and its failure or its fractured initiative to rigidly enforce the rules to contain unfair business practices weaken its position as the regulator of the market irregularities with necessary implications for the consumers and consumerism. Delayed disposal of the cases does not allow the potential victims of deception in the market to be much optimistic. It is true, all the state governments and the non-state consumer organizations are not yet equally keen to make the consumers adequately alert to their rights or make them conversant with the redressal mechanism. It is equally true, non-availability of adequate infrastructural support seriously interrupts efforts to effectively implement the policies and programmes related to consumer welfare at regional and local level. The market is unaccustomed to act as the partner to the initiatives for consumer justice. As it has already been stated, when violation of rules is permitted to be legalized, or, the amount of fine imposed against violation is too small, compared to profit made out of such violation, violation tend to become institutionalized. It is true that ignorance or tolerance or reluctance on the part of the consumers to settle disputes through formal dispute redressal mechanism seriously impedes the progress of consumerism. Truer it is that the poor, the worst victim of deception, everywhere, is arguably endowed with limited choices to resist it.

Strengthening Consumerism

Greater awareness among the consumers about their legitimate rights will make the market more competitive to the advantage of the consumers. With competition within, the market is expected to be more responsive to the needs of the consumers for its own sake. The consumers will gain in terms of quality and price of goods and services. A competitive market acts as an effective regulator of market irregularities. The rationale of increasing interest of the state in promoting consumerism could be to achieve this objective. It could be that the knowledge of the state of its own limitations as a regulator of unfair business practices reinforces its reliance on the 'awakening' of the consumers. It is not enough to 'socialize' the consumers to seek redressal against unscrupulous practices of the market. Unarguably, the state enjoys the legitimacy to pre-empt the deceptive tendencies in the market.

'Consumerism' is not intended to reduce the buyer-seller relationship into one of distrust or, enmity. The business entrepreneur is also a consumer. The position of a consumer makes the business entrepreneur a potential victim of deception in the market. The motivational efforts have to be extended to integrate the business entrepreneurs as the responsible participant to the consumer movement. It is necessary that the inclusive motivational strategy is designed to effectively promote that entitlement to the rights of a consumer is conditioned by uncompromising compliance to lawful and ethical practices as an entrepreneur;

The consumer movement needs to be strengthened with a focus on capacity building of the consumers. The operating Voluntary Consumer Organizations and such other non-profit organizations may act as the crucial partners to the initiatives of the state for promotion of consumerism.

It is our experience that the decisions are delayed beyond the prescribed time limit (particularly the property-related cases; as these cases, more often than not, are referred to the higher forum with an appeal against the Order of the lower forum). The three-tier consumer redressal mechanism, afflicted by large vacant positions and other ills, has to be taken care of for quick disposal of cases, at least, within the statutorily prescribed time-frame. The very objective to provide better protection of the interests of the consumers through unique quasi-judicial grievance redressal mechanism, the basic to the Consumer Protection Act 1986 may otherwise be challenged.

High rate of pendency, processual delay, poor infrastructure are some of the ills which adversely affect the functioning of the forums operating at different levels and the resultant erosion of trust among the consumers in justice delivery system. It is in this context that the role of the National Consumer Helpline is advocated. The National Consumer Helpline provides 'personalized counselling, guidance and information to the aggrieved consumers regarding consumer-related complaints-defective products, deficiency in services and unfair trade'. The complaints are forwarded to 200+ convergence companies for resolution and redress. Should it be that the complaints are not resolved at company level, the consumers are advised to approach the Ombudsman or the Regulator, as applicable. In case, the complaint is not even then resolved, the consumer is further advised to approach the consumer for a further guidance on how and which consumer forum to file complaint (Misra: 2015).

Visits to the district fora in particular reveal that a major problem encountered by the deceived consumers is filing of cases in an appropriate manner. Provision for pre-filing counselling will help the victims of deception (willing to file a case against the unscrupulous trader/service provider).

The voluntary consumer organizations should exist to act as the effective strategic partner of the state in promoting consumer welfare. The state should evolve effective mechanism to 'streamline' the functioning of the voluntary consumer organizations.

Greater involvement of the institutions of higher learning is necessary to relieve the mass of silent sufferings through generation of awareness among them about the rights of consumers, the protective laws, the redressal mechanism and such other issues on regular basis as part of outreach programme.

Notes

1. A *'consumer'* means any person who–
   (i) 'buys any goods for a consideration which has been paid or promised or partly paid and partly promised, or under any system of deferred payment and includes any user of such goods other than the person who buys such goods for consideration paid or promised or partly paid or partly promised, or under any system of deferred payment when such use is made with the approval of such person, but *does not include a person who obtains such goods for resale or for any commercial purpose*'; or,
   (ii) 'hires or avails any services for a consideration which has been paid or promised or partly paid and partly promised, or under any system of deferred payment and includes any beneficiary of such services other than the person who hires or avails of the services for consideration paid or promised, or partly paid and partly promised, or under any system of deferred payment, when such services are availed of with the approval of the first mentioned person *but does not include a person who avails of such services for any commercial purposes*' (Section 2 (1) (d) of The Consumer Protection Act, 1986). See also, Kapoor, Sheetal.
2. *Manu Smriti* is one of the 19 '*Dharmashastras*' ('codes of morals'). It is hailed as the most influential *Smritis* ('that which needs to be remembered'). Unlike the *Vedas*, which are claimed to be of divine origin, the *Smritis* are believed to be the teachings of the legendary personalities to regulate individuals in society (Prasad, 2008); Islam (2008).
3. 'Grade designation mark' consists of Agmark labels of different types e.g. tie-on-labels, paste-on-labels, banderol labels. Each label-type carries letters indicating series and serial number [General Grading and Marking Rules 1988 (as amended up to 1991), www.agmarknet.nic.in/gmr1988.htm]

4. See, General Grading and Marking Rules 1988 (as amended up to 1991), www.agmarknet.nic.in/gmr1988.htm
5. See, General Grading and Marking Rules 1988 (as amended up to 1991), www.agmarknet.nic.in/gmr1988.htm
6. With effect from 27 July 1964; See, The Drugs and Cosmetics Act, 1940
7. The Monopolies and Restrictive Trade Practices Act, 1969, yet another important Act, had been enacted to deal with unfair trade practices. The MRTP Act has been repealed and replaced by the Competition Act 2002 (with effect from 1 September 2009). It was decided that the MRTP Commission 'will continue to exercise its jurisdiction and power under the repealed MRTP Act in respect of any case or proceeding filed before 1 September 2009, for a period of two years'. On or after 1 September 2009, no new case will be entertained by the Commission. All pending cases related to Unfair Trade Practices will be transferred to the National Commission, constituted under the Consumer Protection Act, 1986. The National Commission may transfer any case that it deems fit, to a State Commission, constituted under the Consumer Protection Act, 1986.

   Another legislative initiative, which has recently been introduced in the form of a Bill to protect the interests of the potential consumers in the housing market and is awaiting approval of the Parliament, must be mentioned. The title of the Bill is 'The Real Estate (Regulation and Development) Bill, 2013'. The Bill has been designed to protect the interest of the potential consumers in the housing sector through promotion of fair play in real estate transactions and ensuring timely execution of housing projects. The Bill provides for a uniform regulatory environment, speedy adjudication of disputes and orderly growth of the real estate sector. It is hoped that the proposed Act will ensure greater accountability and significantly reduce frauds and delays. Greater accountability and transparency in real estate will allow the sector to become eligible for access to capital and financial market for its long-term orderly growth (PIB: 2013). Some of the major features of the proposed Act may be mentioned.

   (i) *Applicability of the Proposed Bill:* The proposed Bill limited in its applicability. It is applicable only to residential real estate i.e. housing and any other independent use ancillary to housing.

   (ii) *Regulatory Authority:* The Bill has provision for establishment of one or more 'Real Estate Regulatory Authority' in each state/UT, or one Authority for two or more states/UT, by the appropriate government, with specified functions, powers, and responsibilities to exercise oversight of real estate transactions, to appoint adjudicating officers, to settle disputes between the parties involved, and to impose penalty and interest.

(iii) *Mandatory Disclosure:* Apart from registration of real estate projects and real estate agents, there is provision for mandatory public disclosure of details of the registered projects including the land status, carpet area, number of the apartments booked and status of the statutory approvals.

(iv) *Fast Track Dispute Redressal Mechanism:* The Bill includes provision for establishment of fast track dispute resolution mechanisms for settlement of disputes, through adjudicating officers (an officer not below the rank of Joint Secretary to the state government) to be appointed by the authority.

(v) *Real Estate Appellate Tribunal:* In order to ensure speedy adjudication of disputes, the Bill has provision for establishment of an Appellate Tribunal to hear appeals from the orders of the Authority and the adjudicating officer.

(vi) Punitive Provisions: In case of contravention of the provisions of the Bill or the orders of the Authority or the Tribunal, the proposed legislation includes Punitive provisions including de-registration of the project and penalties.

(vii) Rights and duties of the buyers: The buyers in the housing market will enjoy the privilege to secure information pertaining to the property booked, to know stage-wise time schedule of project completion, claim possession of the apartment or plot or building as per promoter declaration, refund with interest in case of default by the promoter, and after possession entitled to necessary documents and plans. The buyers will also be under legal obligation to make necessary payments and carry out other responsibilities as per the agreement.

8. For details, see http://business.gov.in/consumer_rights/education_awareness.php and http://www.consumereducation.in
9. For details, see www.consumer-voice.org/News
10. For details, see www.consumersinternational.org
11. 'From 2007–08 to 2011–12, the monthly per-capita consumption expenditure (MPCE) in rural areas increased at a compound annual rate of 16.7 per cent, compared with 15.6 per cent in urban centres, shows the consumer expenditure survey of the National Sample Survey Organization (NSSO)' (Business Standard: 2014).
12. While emphasizing on consumer education for improving the level of awareness among the consumers in India, the sub-group on Consumer Awareness and Education of the Working Group

(2012–17) noted that the concept of consumer education is poorly understood in India. The sub-group thought that 'a holistic policy for consumer education and better re-sourcing of activities geared towards consumer education is needed'. Apart from looking at international best practices, the main stake-holders viz. government departments, industry, consumer groups, education and advice providers, interest groups and community agencies need to work together. (See, Part II, Twelfth Plan Strategy, Consumer Education, p. 76).

References

APGM (1937): The Agricultural Produce (Grading and Marking) Act, 1937 (as amended up to 1991).
www.agmarknet.nic.in/std-gra.htm;
www.agmarknet.nic.in/gmr1988.htm

Balkrishnan, Pulapre (2007): 'The Recovery of India: Economic Growth in the Nehru Era', *Economic and Political Weekly*, V. XLII, Nos. 45 and 46.

Business Line (2014): 'Urbanites Lack Awareness about Consumer Rights: Survey', *The Hindu*, 15 March.
http://www.thehindubusinessline.com/economy/urbanites-lack-awareness-about-consumer-rights- survey/article5788894.ece

Business Standard (2014): 'Rural India Tops Consumption Charts', 3 April 2014.

Business Today (2002): 'Down The Long Road to Consumer Justice', 20 January.

Business Today (2013): 'Govt. looks at easing FDI norms for real estate', 5 August.

CCS (2014): Centre for Consumer Studies, Indian Institute of Public Administration, New Delhi

CPA (1986): The Consumer Protection Act, 1986.
www.ncdrc.nic.in/1_1.html

CUTS (2012): State of the Indian Consumer 2012, CUTS, Centre for Consumer Action, Research and Training (CART).
www.CUTS-International.org/CART/consumersup/pdf/Report_state_of_the_Indian_consumer–2012, pdf

Dash, Dipak K. (2014): 'Consumer Protection Movement Faltering', *Times of India*, 16 November.

DCA (1940): The Drugs and Cosmetics Act, 1940 (Corrected up to April 2003), Ministry of Health and Family Welfare, GOI.
www.cdsco.nic.in/html/copy%20of%201.%20d&cact121.pdf

Economic Times (2013): 'Rise in Credit and Debit Cards Spending Signals India's Transformation into Cashless Economy', E T Bureau, 6 October.

http://articles.economictimes.indiatimes.com/2013-10-06/news/42745678_1_credit-cards-debit-card-payments

EY-FICCIEY-FICCI (2012): Bribery and Corruption: Ground Reality in India, FICCI, Ernst and Young

Galanter, Marc (1997): *Law and Society in Modern India*, Oxford University Press (as quoted in Prasad (2008).

IPC (1860): Indian Penal Code, 1860

Islam, Sayem (2008): 'The Arthasastra: Insights on Statecraft and Reflections of Ancient Indian Society'.
www.umich.edu/~historyj /docs/2008-winter/islam.pdf

Kapoor, Sheetal: Consumer and the Market, *Monograph*, Center for Consumer Studies, Indian Institute of Public Administration, New Delhi

KPMG (2011): India Survey on Bribery and Corruption, Retrieved from www.kpmg.com/IN/en/services/.../Bribery_Survey_Report_Final.pdf

Law Commission (1958): Eighth Report (Sale of Goods Act, 1930), Law Commission of India, Ministry of Law, GOI (Chairman: M. C. Setalvad)

Misra, Suresh (2015): 'Consumer Grievance Redressal Mechanism: The Role of National Consumer Helpline (NCH)', Paper presented at National Seminar on 'Consumer Justice in Globalizing India: Challenges and Choices' organized by the Department of Sociology, University of Kalyani in collaboration with Centre for Consumer Studies, Indian Institute of Public Administration, New Delhi (November 19-20).

Mukhopadhyay, Asish and Paul, Karunamayee (2010): 'Shaping of Consumerism: Performance and Challenges of Voluntary Consumer Organizations', Consumer Protection and Globalization, Center for Consumer Studies, Indian Institute of Public Administration, New Delhi and Kalasalingam University, TN.

Narayanswamy, Srinivasa (1999): 'The Milestones of Consumer Movement' in *The Hindu* Folio, 31 October.

Naz, Humera (2010): 'Price Control Policy of Allauddin Khalji: Achievement or Failure', *JHSS*, Vol. 1, No: 2, pp. 68-84.

NCDRC: National Consumer Disputes Redressal Commission.
http://ncdrc.nic.in/

Panta, Murali Prasad (2001): *Business, Consumer and the Government*, Mittal Publications, New Delhi.

Patil, Ashok (2011): 'A Study on Consumer Production through Maintenance of Product Safety and Standard in India', Asian Law Institute Working Paper Series No: 23, Asian Law Institute, National University of Singapore.
www.law.nus.edu.sg.asli/pdf/WPS023.pdf

Paul, Karunamayee (2010): 'Protecting Rights of Consumers: Exploring role of state and non-state consumer organizations in West Bengal', Unpublished Ph.D. Dissertation, Department of Sociology, University of Kalyani.

PIB (2013): 'Real Estate Bill to Protect the Interest of the Consumers and Promote Fair Play in Real Estate Transactions', Press Information Bureau, Ministry of Housing and Urban Poverty Alleviation, GOI, 5 June.

Prasad (2008): 'Historical Evolution of Consumer Protection and Law in India', *Journal of Texas Consumer Law*.
www.hexconsumerlaw.com/ V11N3/JCCL_India.pdf

Rangarajan, L.N. (2010): *Kautilya: The Arthashastra*, Digital Edition, Penguin, New Delhi.

RBI (2015): Annual Report on Banking Ombudsman Scheme, 2013–14 (see Table 7 of the Report), Reserve Bank of India.

Report (2012–17): Report of the Working Group on Consumer Protection, Twelfth Plan (2012–17), Vol. II, Department of Consumer Affairs, Ministry of Consumer Affairs, Food and Public Distribution, GOI.
http://planningcommission.gov.in/aboutus/committee/wrkgrp12/pp/wg_cp2.pdf

Seetharaman, P. and Sethi, Mohini. (2002): *Consumerism-Strategies and Tactics*, CBS Publishers, New Delhi.

SGA (1930): The Sale of Goods Act, 1930 (See Section 12 and Section 16), See also, Patil (2011); Prasad (2008).

Singh, S.S. and Chadah, Sapna: 'Consumer Protection in India: Some Reflections', *Monograph*, Centre for Consumer Studies, Indian Institute of Public Administration, New Delhi.

Times of India (2013): 'Average Credit Card Spend Increases 42 per cent in Two Years', 23 July.

Times of India (2014), 'Centre to Amend Consumer Protection Act', 14 November.

Verma, D.P.S. (2002): 'Development in Consumer Protection in India', *Journal of Consumer Policy*, V.25, No. 1, March.

CHAPTER 4

Urban Housing Market

Vulnerability and Choices of Consumers

Presumably, a consumer suffers most when the market is speculative, exploitative, non-transparent and left to operate with no authority to regulate the market-irregularities. The urban housing market in India is a case in point. The buyers, in course of buying a property, ordinarily experience a host of tricky practices which are neither avoidable nor acceptable to them. These are either ignored or, negotiated or, contested by the consumers. All such practices do not qualify as 'dispute', always. The deceptive tendencies in the housing market persist for a variety of reasons including ignorance or reluctance to fight or tolerance to such practices on the part of the consumers.

Introduction

For centuries, the cities, despite undying constraints, have been the centres of promises: of trade, finance and economic, politics, specialized skill and services, architecture, culture, learning and innovation, modernity, aspirations, freedom and protest. The move to urban living thus continues and across the globe in quest of opportunities and an improved quality of life. Urbanization in India has been taking place faster than anticipated. The number of cities with population of more than 1 million increased from 35 to 53, of which eight cities have a population of more than 5 million. In coming couple of decades, urbanization will be more widespread. It will spread across India impacting upon all her states. Projections are that by 2030, out of a total population of 1.4 billion, over 575 million people may be living in urban areas (Survey, 2014–15: 105).

While the cities already matter, India's economic future will depend more on her cities. The cities have become the centres of the new-age economy comprising the technology-intensive IT/ITES, Financial Services including banking and insurance and other services. These centres are drawing the skilled manpower from across the country. The ICT revolution has facilitated gendered shift in migration to the centres of new-age economy. Women are migrating to these locations, in greater number and 'independent of marriage-related re-location', to join the gender-inclusive new-age economy. The cities in India are already witnessing fair presence of middle class households and a new wave of consumption. It is estimated, 'the middle class[1] will dominate the cities by 2025 when about three-quarters of India's urbanites will be part of middle class, compared with just more than one-tenth today' (McKinsey, 2007: 56).

It is obvious that the new urban consumers will have an impact well beyond sales of goods and services. Rapidly growing cities in developing economies have been facing a complex and challenging task in keeping pace with their expanding population and rising expectations. The cities in India are no exception. Rapid urbanization accompanied by growth of households with decent disposable income are going to put tremendous pressure on already overburdened infrastructure and housing in particular in urban India.

The residential segment makes the maximum contribution to the real estate sector and enjoys the largest part of its market share. The residential segment space is consumed by affordable, mid-income and luxury housing. It has already been indicated that the urban affordable segment (EWS/LIG category) demands sincere attention and where participation of the private sector seems necessary, considering the fact that the mobilization of required resources by the state may be difficult and more so, if the commitment 'Housing for All' by 2022 is to be honoured. It is expected that relaxation in FDI norms together with initiatives of the state, as it has already been stated, will ease the situation.

As evident from Table 26, the urban India suffers from shortage of housing of all categories (including the middle income and high income groups). The gap between demand and supply of this category of housing units is widening and the price of housing units is on the rise. National Housing Bank's RESIDEX (city-wise housing price index) indicate that in 2014, out of 26 cities, 17 witnessed increase in prices over 2013 (Survey, 2014–15: 118). The demand of this segment of housing units has been steadily growing.[2]

A significant proportion of mid-income households (with an average annual income between ₹ 5 lakhs and ₹ 10 lakhs per annum) reside in the urban areas. The top six viz. New Delhi, Mumbai, Chennai, Kolkata, Hyderabad and Bangalore, it is argued, witnessed the bulk of economic activities in the first phase of growth. The next phase of growth will see the emergence of Tier II and Tier III cities as centres of economic activities and these include: Surat, Nagpur, Vadodara, Jaipur, Vishakhapatnam and Kochi. The point is, with the expansion of economic activities (and particularly IT/ITES sector) in these Tier II and Tier III cities, the supply of middle income housing units, (typically 2/3 BHK and measuring about 800–1,200 square feet) will outstrip the demand (*The Indian Express*, 2015). The expansion of emerging sectors to the Tier II and Tier III cities (already in progress) attracts young and skilled manpower to these locations from across the country. This new generation of migrant professionals (usually the first-time home-buyer) is the prime target of the urban mid-income residential real estate sector. The price of a housing unit (measuring between 800–1,200 sq. ft.) varies between ₹ 25 lakhs and ₹ 60 lakhs depending upon the type of city, locality and amenities. NHB's RESIDEX shows that housing price is on the rise in Tier II cities, as well.

Real estate has been an integral part of the emerging markets. The burgeoning urban middle class with disposable income, diminishing household size, easy accessibility to home loan from Housing Finance Companies[3] on 'affordable' terms, policy initiatives of the state for the growth of the real estate sector, incentives (exemption in tax on income) to the buyers and one's perception of home as a need or an asset or simply fulfillment of desire are the major factors leading to increasing demand for construction of mid-income housing units in all categories of towns.

In India, the urban residential segment is highly fragmented. The organized segment of the urban housing market is represented by the large builders and developers and government or government-affiliated enterprises with a share of 30 per cent of the business. The unorganized sector, which builds about 70 per cent of total housing units constructed, comprises the small builders and developers and contractors. The segment is largely unregulated. And, there is absence of professionalism, standardization and protection of consumers. These impede healthy growth of the urban residential segment (Parliament, 2014: 8).[4]

Presumably, a consumer suffers most when the market is speculative, exploitative, non-transparent and left to operate with no authority to regulate the market irregularities. The urban housing market in India is a case in point. The buyers, in course of buying a property, ordinarily experience a host of tricky practices which are neither avoidable nor acceptable to them. The consumers respond to these practices in three different ways. These are either ignored or negotiated or contested. The decision to contest is mediated through any or a combination of social, economic and psychological variables. All such practices which are encountered by the consumers, do not qualify as 'dispute', always. The deceptive tendencies in the housing market persist.

The acute shortage of affordable housing, from which the urban India chronically suffers, has tragic implications for the consumers. It is tragic because the urgent need for comfortable living reinforced by a feeling of 'powerlessness' vis-à-vis the knowledge of events around interferes with the buyer's decision to approach the dispute redressal mechanism for resolution. More often than not, the consumers tend to ignore the market-irregularities unless otherwise compelled. It is well argued that deception in everyday-life-situation has become so 'widespread and deep that the society instead of complaining and fighting for it has started accepting it' (Bana, 2006: 3). The vulnerability of the consumers to fraudulent practices in the urban housing market and its prevention have, however, failed to attract adequate attention of the social researchers undertaking empirical studies with respect to housing market in urban India. This is despite the fact that the incidence of deception in the urban housing market has been increasing, alarmingly. A sector-wise distribution of the complaints filed (since inception) in Bengaluru District Forum

(Urban) and Karnataka State Consumer Disputes Redressal Commission reveals that the housing sector tops the list with 4,295 and 744 cases, respectively. Given the neo-liberal bent of the state and its occasional fraudulent behaviour as the promoter of housing complexes, the efforts of the state in pre-empting the probable sources of unscrupulous practices in urban housing market do not allow the consumers to be much optimistic.

The present segment seeks to address three major issues. These are, first, what are the tricky practices, termed as 'critical issues' for the present purpose, encountered and experienced by the consumers in the urban housing market? Second, how do the consumers negotiate those critical issues? Finally, why do deceptive tendencies persist in the urban housing market? These and such other issues have been addressed in the following pages based on empirically derived data from two cities viz. Bengaluru and Kolkata.[5]

Critical Issues

The consumers in urban housing market frequent a series of 'critical issues'. These are critical because the consumers neither avoid nor accept these practices. The number of 'registered disputes', however, do not actually reveal the magnitude of close encounters of the consumers with such issues as these do not always mature as 'dispute' requiring formal institutional intervention. As it will be evident, response of the consumers to the 'critical issues' is not uniform, either. Individual difference in response is influenced by one's affordability of damage/loss caused by deception and/or, one's own assessment of self to withstand the probable 'costs' associated with resolution through formal dispute redressal mechanism.

The expression 'critical issues', for the present purpose, refer to the issues, which are encountered and perceived by the consumers in the urban housing market as amounting to breach of contract and/or, deficiency in service and/or, willful neglect or non-compliance to promises and/or, contrary to legitimate expectations leading to personal miseries/sufferings (Mukhopadhyay: 2014). There is no reason to believe that every consumer, negotiating with the urban housing market, experience all the 'critical issues' as revealed through the present study. As few 'critical issues' are more common than others, the 'critical issues' may thus be distributed based on the frequency of encounters or the commonalities of experiences of the consumers. Moreover, the 'critical issues' may be distributed in terms of the type of issue involved viz. financial, service and ownership.

Majority of the buyers purchased flat/apartment from the private builders/developers. While some bought from joint venture companies (with State Housing Board) few bought housing built by the State Housing Board/Housing Cooperatives. The price of the flat of first two categories was higher compared to the last mentioned category. However, not all those who had purchased flat/apartment made the first payment at a specific stage of construction of their respective housing unit. It is usual that any housing project built by private promoters carries with it some incentives (concessional rate in floor price) to the buyers at pre-launch stage. It is usual that a reputed builder/developer, with a housing project in a good locality attracts buyers even before the construction actually takes off. Those who bought flat from the private builders/promoters owners made the first payment at different stage of construction of respective housing unit. None of the respondents, however, took the risk of paying the builder/developer before the construction of the housing project actually took off (i.e.; pre-launch stage). This was despite the fact that attraction of pre-launch (special) discount was there. The majority (153: 54.64%) of the buyers, who bought flat/apartment from the private builders, made the first payment while the flat/apartment was 'under construction', followed by those (73: 26.07%) who made the first payment when the construction was 'near complete'. Others (54: 19.28%) made the first payment when the flat/apartment was in a 'ready to move in' position.[6] The prime consideration for buying an under construction housing unit has been found to be the price of the housing unit. With the progress in construction, the cost of the unit increases. Those who made the first payment, while the unit was under construction, were adequately alert about the reputation of the builder/developer in terms of completion of the project as per schedule. In some cases, the risk was relatively low as the builders were small and personally known to the buyers. In case of a housing unit built by the state housing board or, by a housing co-operative, the buyers had no choice in terms of payment of first installment. The buyers had to pay as and when demand for payment of 'call money' would be made depending upon the progress of construction excepting the provision of 'Application Money'. It was noted that in case of housing built by the private builders, the initial payment, known as 'Booking Fee', is negotiable.

The decision of the buyers in regard to purchase of the housing unit was influenced by a number of considerations. The buyers were asked to identify top five reasons which provided the bases of their choice of this particular housing unit. Affordability was accorded primacy over others. This was followed by other considerations, (as prioritized by the buyers themselves), reputation of the builder/developer, locality, connectivity and time to be taken for completion. Also, there were other considerations like position of the flat, acquaintance with other buyers of the same housing complex, distance from place of work, distance of school for kids and distance of the market place.

Most of the buyers, being the first-time buyers of housing unit, had no prior personal experiences of 'critical issues'. Majority of them were, however, aware of prevalence of fraudulent practices in the real estate market. Few learnt about fraudulent practices in the real estate market from close kin/friend who were victims of such practices. There was an agreement among the owners of flat/apartment that the 'critical issues' are not avoidable. Such practices are unacceptable, as well. It is important to note that most of the buyers were aware that there were legal remedies against non-compliance to commitments on the part of the builders. Yet, their response to the 'critical issues', as it has already been said, were not uniform.

The 'critical issues' may be broadly classified as: pre-possession and post-possession. These may further be distributed as: financial, legal, service and miscellaneous. It is wrong to assume that all critical issues are encountered by all the consumers in the urban residential market. But, it has been recorded that there has been variation in frequency of occurrence or in commonality in experiences of the buyers. Hence, based on frequency of occurrence or, commonality in experience of the home-buyers, the critical issues may further be distributed as: most frequent, frequent and infrequent. A microscopic minority of the respondents, who indicated that they did not encounter any problem worth mentioning, agreed to distribute the issues in terms of frequency of occurrences based on their perception.

The pre-possession 'critical issues', as identified by the buyers, are: (1) Bargaining over price of the housing unit; (2) Non-refund/unusual delay in refund of 'Booking Fee' against cancellation of 'Booking'; (3) Access to legal documents related to the property for verification which was available only upon payment of requisite 'Booking fee'; (4) A part of the 'booking fee' (not uniform) was deducted before refund was made in case of cancellation of booking of the flat and that too, even when the buyer was not at fault; (5) Delayed delivery of the flat; (6) Non-payment of compensation for delayed delivery of the flat citing reasons beyond the control of the developer/builder; (7) Change in floor plan without the consent of the buyer; (8) Escalation in price of the flat on flimsy grounds and the most common being the hike in price of raw materials and hiring charges of labour; (9) Difficulties associated with the 'Completion Certificate'; (10) Difficulties associated with home loan from Housing Finance Companies (HFC) for non-availability of valid documents from the seller regarding the property on sale.

The post-possession 'critical issues' are: (1) Unauthorized construction; (2) Poor quality of material used for construction; (3) Problem associated with super-built-area and carpet area; (4) Delay in transfer of electric metre in the name of the buyer; (5) Delay in conversion of electric connection from commercial to domestic; (6) Delay in registration of property/khata transfer; (7) Non-compliance or, partial compliance to commitments (particularly amenities).

As it has already been stated, based on frequency of occurrence or, commonality in experience of the home-buyers, the critical issues may further be distributed as: most frequent, frequent and infrequent.

Most frequent 'critical issues' are: (1) Delayed delivery of flat/apartment; (2) Non-payment of compensation for delay in delivery of housing unit; (3) Poor quality of material used in construction; (4) Non-compliance/partial compliance to commitments (interior fittings) proposed in the brochure; (5) Problem associated with super-built-area, carpet area and common area.

Frequently encountered 'critical issues' are: (1) Delay in registration of property/khata transfer; (2) Unauthorized construction; (3) Non-compliance/partial compliance to commitments regarding amenities proposed in the brochure; (4) Non-refund/delay in refund of 'booking fee' against cancellation; (5) Bargaining over price of the flat; (6) Escalation in price of the flat on flimsy ground.

Less frequent 'critical issues' are: (1) Difficulties associated with the 'completion certificate'; (2) Difficulties associated with securing home loan from HFCs for non-availability of valid documents from the seller regarding the property on sale; (3) Change in floor plan without consent of the buyer.

Negotiating Critical Issues

How do the consumers respond to the 'critical issues'? While individual difference in response to the issues has been noted, the consumers have limited choices. The source of individual difference in response may be found rooted deep into difference in subjective understanding of one's affordability to damage/loss caused by deception and/or, one's own assessment of self to withstand the probable 'costs' associated with resolution through formal redressal mechanism. Generally speaking, the consumers tend to ignore a 'critical issue' until the loss/damage caused is well within one's own construct of 'affordable' limit. Beyond this point, the consumer becomes eager for a settlement through an intermediary, if necessary. A consumer decides to contest the issue either in an appropriate consumer forum or, in a court of law, only when any such initiative fails to yield desired result.

The decision of the consumers to contest in an appropriate consumer forum or, in a court of law is mediated by a host of considerations. These are: one's (a) location in the socio-economic hierarchy; (b) capacity to endure the 'costs' associated with a legal dispute; (c) notion of self vis-à-vis the adversary; (d) anticipation of outcome in case of litigation. That possible delay in disposal of a property-related dispute in particular has discouraging effect for the victim of deception was endorsed by most of the respondents.

Drawing cue from above, it may be argued, all 'critical issues', which the buyers encounter, do not actually qualify as 'dispute'. Again, the respondents reported that an out-of-court settlement of a 'dispute' is always encouraged. Also, out-of-court settlement is by and large preferred by the parties to a dispute for a variety of reasons and chiefly to avoid the probable 'costs' associated with in-court settlement. Thus, a case is filed only when an effort towards a mutually acceptable out-of-court settlement fails. The point that we wish to make is that the cases, which are eventually filed at consumer disputes redressal forum (at various levels), do not actually reveal the magnitude of encounters of the consumers with unethical business practices in India. Again, it is evident that a consumer, even when he is not ignorant about the redressal mechanism or, do not suffer from lack of faith on it, prefers out-of-court negotiation to resolution according to due process of law. Moreover, the decision of a consumer to seek institutional intervention for favourable resolution of a 'dispute' is likely to be interfered by a range of considerations including uncertainties about outcome of the dispute and tine to be taken for resolution of the dispute.

Apprehension of possible delay in disposal of property-related cases in particular has been found to be the most prominent reason that discourages a consumer to stay away from formal redressal mechanism, unless otherwise impelled. It has been recorded that a significant number of cases filed against the builder/promoter is referred to the higher Forum in the form of an Appeal against the Order of a lower Forum. Available data from the Karnataka State Consumer Disputes Redressal Commission (Bengaluru) suggest that there were (as on 31 August 2012) as many as 3,370 cases of Appeals against the private builders. The number of Appeals against the government was 834. In fact, a review of the state of disposal of cases does not appear to be encouraging as a good number of registered cases (dispute) are not disposed within specified time norms. The available data from the West Bengal State Consumer Dispute Redressal Commission (Kolkata) on state of disposal of cases (as on June 2012) demonstrate that 3,304 cases (43.22%) were only disposed off within time norms out of 7,644 cases (filed after 15 March 2003).

Persistence of Deception

The respondents attributed persistence of deception in the urban housing market to four probable sources. The probable *(four)* sources, put in order of rank assigned by the consumers, are: (1) Political patronization/tolerance to deceptive tendencies in the market; (2) Chronic shortage of urban housing; (3) State's limited success in pre-empting irregularities in real estate segment; ignorance/reluctance/tolerance on the part of the consumers to deceptive market practices.

Deception in urban housing market, as endorsed by the respondents, is not alone a function of chronic shortage of housing that increases the opportunities for speculation. It is associated with governance, as well. Again, the compelling need or indomitable desire for housing in a scarce market allows the deceptive tendencies to prevail. Moreover, ignorance and/or inadequate interest or reluctance 'to fight deception' on the part of the victims of deception do not allow the deceptive tendencies to die. What could be the appropriate strategies to reduce the deceptive tendencies to unavoidable minimal in urban housing market?

A regulatory authority is only essential to make the urban housing market transparent and accountable. Failing this, deception in urban housing market will continue with 'costs' to the buyers.

There are rules to check deceptive behaviour of the market. What is required is a vigilant state committed to rigid enforcement of such rules. If the society permits violations of building rules to be legalized, or, the amount of fine imposed for such violations is too small compared to profit made out of violations, then violations tend to be institutionalized. Securing corporate accountability becomes difficult.

Apparently small issues like 'carpet area', 'common area' create confusion as these terms are not clearly defined. These need to be defined in clear terms and be part of the sale agreement and sale deed. It is to be ensured that the deal is transparent.

Enhancing trust of the consumers about the dispute redressal mechanism is essential. One possible way of enhancing trust of the consumers about the redressal mechanism could be to introduce fast track dispute redressal mechanism for the housing sector.

Ultimately, of course, the issue of reducing deception is linked to political will. Passage of the Real Estate (Development and Regulation) Act, unaccompanied by commensurate political decision, is possibly based on certain myopia.

Notes

1. Following the methodology adopted by National Council of Applied Economic Research (NCAER), the middle class has been defined as 'household with a disposable incomes of ₹ 2,00,000 to ₹ 10,00,000 a

year in real 2,000 terms. That seems quite low in the context of a developed country but because the cost of living is lower in India this range of income buys a recognizably middle class life-style' (see footnote 5, McKinsey, 2007: 56). What constitutes the middle class continues to be debated. Scholars differ over the income-based definition of the 'not poor but not-rich' class in developing countries. Estimate of the size of urban middle class in India also varies (Meyer and Birdsall, 2012: 2; Shukla, 2010: 101).

2. According to one estimate, the mid-income housing market is expected to account for 7 per cent of the total housing demand till 2,028 which is 3–3.5 million houses (KPMG, 2014: 9).
3. Borrowers' type-wise Disbursement Trend of Housing Loans by Housing Finance Companies suggests that individuals comprised 84 per cent among the borrowers in 2012. Again, the number of individuals taking home loan above 25 lakhs increased from 29,348 (43.02% of total) in 2012 to 43,712 (47.21% of total) in 2013 (NHB, 2013).
4. As it has already been stated, the Real Estate (Regulation and Development) Bill, 2013, intends to ensure consumer protection, establishing regulatory bodies at Centre and states for ethical and transparent business practices in the real estate sector. The Real Estate (Regulation and Development) Bill, 2013, was first introduced in Parliament in August, 2013. The said Bill was referred to the standing committee, which submitted the report in February 2014. Some of the recommendations of the Standing Committee (hereafter Committee) are:
   - (i) Apart from the residential real estate, the Committee recommends that the Bill will regulate commercial and industrial real estate.
   - (ii) The Bill excludes projects smaller than 1,000 square metres or 12 apartments from its purview. The Committee recommends reducing the limit to 100 sq mt and three apartments to include the large number of small housing project within the jurisdiction of the Bill.
   - (iii) The Bill defined 'carpet area' as the net usable floor area of an apartment, excluding the area covered by the walls. The Committee recommends that the 'net usable floor area shall mean to include the area sold to the allottee for his individual use, which includes living room, bedroom, kitchen area, lavatory(s), bathroom(s), balcony/verandah if covered, any area for the residence of domestic help within the apartment, and covered parking or any other type of independent use ancillary to the purpose specified'.

(iv) The Committee recommends that mentioning of 'common area' in sale agreement and sale deed will remove the scope of any ambiguity.

(v) The Committee recommends that the 'construction execution certificate' should be included in the Bill to ensure better development of the project and fix responsibility of the promoters/builders in clear terms.

(vi) The Committee desires that the Model Agreement should include the provision regarding the quality of materials and technology that would be used at different stages of construction. Also, it should be obligatory for the Real Estate Regulatory Authority to ensure strict compliance of the Rules and regular monitoring of the same.

(vii) The Committee desires that the antecedents of the promoters should be checked before registering the projects (in lieu of promoters' companies) being promoted by them. If the activities of the promoters are not found fit, then the project should not be registered. Further, the promoter should also be blacklisted for doing any further business across the country after two such defaults (PRS, 2014; Parliament, 2014).

The Real Estate (Regulation and Development) Act, 2016 received the assent of the President of India on the 25 March 2016 (*Gazette of India*, 2016).

5. The relevant data had been drawn from both sources: the primary and the secondary. The empirical data has been drawn in a number of spells. The initial spell of fieldwork had been carried out with the intention to pre test the questionnaire/schedule. Informal discussion with the functionaries of the Karnataka State Consumer Dispute Redressal Commission and the West Bengal State Consumer Redressal Commission and significant others were of much help. It was originally planned that the intensive fieldwork for the study would be carried out, in spells, in two urban residential areas. These were: viz. White Field and New Town, located in the eastern fringes of Bengaluru and Kolkata, respectively. Later, Dumdum, another city-fringe (of Kolkata), was included as part of the study. The relevant primary data had been drawn from this residential locality also. The first two study areas, viz.; White Field and New Town are upcoming residential areas and in close proximity to the IT/ITES hub of respective cities. These residential localities are numerically dominated by those who are associated with the IT/ITES/service sector industry, often called, the 'new-age economy'. In White Field, a good number of (private) builders' apartments either have been completed or are near completion. In New Town, it has been found, some apartments are coming up under public-private partnership

(PPP). Dumdum, on the other hand, is relatively an old and a congested area and small investors are engaged in building ownership flats. A good many of the buyers were attracted to this locality mainly because of relatively low cost of housing and good connectivity including the metro rail. The owners, who have recently (not earlier than five years) moved in to their respective flat/apartment after buying the same from the private builder/State Housing Board/joint venture company, constitute the sample. It was assumed that this category of buyers/residents must have developed fair knowledge about the current state of urban housing market as they themselves have passed through the process of negotiation with the market.

The relevant primary data were drawn through pre-tested, structured schedule. As already indicated, informal interviews/meetings had been arranged with (i) the Functionaries of the Urban District Forum (Bengaluru and Kolkata) (ii) the Functionaries of the State Consumer Disputes Redressal Commission of respective states (iii) the Functionaries of the operating Resident Welfare Organizations (iv) the Functionaries of the NGOs and significant others. These Informal meetings/interviews provided useful insights. It was ultimately decided that the size of the sample would be kept limited to 280 chiefly for probing interaction with the respondents for a better understanding of the issues in the inquiry.

6. A recent survey carried out by an online property portal among 1,511 first time home buyers from across the country suggests that the first-time buyers prefer 'ready-to-move-in' to 'under-construction' housing unit. Most participants were male and in the age group of 28–45 years. Repeated delays in completion of construction and other issues deter the first time buyers from buying property under construction. (*Express*: 2014).

References

Bana, Ravindra (2006): 'Housing and Consumer', *Monograph*, Indian Institute of Public Administration, New Delhi.

Express (2015): 'Emerging Trends: Tier II, III Cities Set to Grow in Next Phase of Economic Boom', *The Indian Express*, 14 February

Express (2014): 'First-time-buyers prefer Ready-to-move-in flat', *The New Indian Express*, 23 August. http://www.newindianexpress.com/cities/bengaluru/First-Time-Buyers-Prefer-Ready-to-Move-in-Flats/2014/08/23/article2394049.ece

Gazette of India (2016): The Gazette of India, Extraordinary, Part II, No. 17, Saturday, 26 March, Ministry of Law and Justice, New Delhi.

KPMG (2014): Indian Real Estate-Opening Doors, KPMG-NAREDCO

McKinsey (2007): 'Tracking the Growth of India's Middle Class', *McKinsey Quarterly*, Number 3.
https://genesis.iitm.ac.in/downloads/resources/startup/tracking%20the%20growth%20of%20indian%20middle%20class.pdf

McKinsey (2010): India's Urban Awakening: Building Inclusive Cities, Sustaining Economic Growth, McKinsey Global Institute.

McKinsey (2012): Urban World: Cities and the Rise of the Consuming Class, McKinsey Global Institute, June.

Meyer, Christian and Birdsall, Nancy (2012): 'New Estimates of India's Middle Class', Center for Global Development, Peterson Institute for International Economics, pp. 1–10.

Mukhopadhyay, Asish (2014): 'Negotiating Unethical Business Practices: Consumers in Urban Housing Market' *International Journal of Business Ethics in Developing Societies*, Vol. 3, Issue 1, pp. 1–7.

NHB (2013): Report on Trend and Progress of Housing in India, 2013, National Housing Bank.
http://www.nhb.org.in/Whats_new/Report-on-Trend-and-Progress-of-Housing-in-India–2013.pdf

Parliament (2014): Report of the Standing Committee on Urban Development ('The Real Estate (Regulation and Development) Bill, 2013'), Ministry of Housing and Urban Poverty Alleviation (Presented to Lok Sabha on 17–02–2014).
http://www.prsindia.org/uploads/media/Real%20Estate/SCR-Real%20Estate%20Bill.pdf

PRS (2014): Standing Committee Report Summary (The Real Estate (Regulation and Development) Bill, 2013), PRS Legislative Research.
http://www.prsindia.org/uploads/media/Real%20Estate/SCR%20Summary-%20Real%20Estate%20Bill.pdf

Shukla, R. (2010): How India Earns, Spends and Saves: Unmasking the Real India, SAGE and NCAER-CMCR, New Delhi.

Survey (2014): Economic Survey, 2014–15, Vol. II, Union Budget, Ministry of Finance, GOI.
http://indiabudget.nic.in/es2014–15/echapter- vol2.pdf

Index